WICKED SHARP

A Born Bad Novel

MEGHAN O'FLYNN

PYGMALION
PUBLISHING

WICKED SHARP

Distributed by Pygmalion Publishing, LLC

ISBN (electronic): 978-1-947748-26-2

ISBN (print): 978-1-947748-27-9

WANT MORE FROM MEGHAN?

There are many more books to choose from!

Learn more about Meghan's novels on

https://meghanoflynn.com

For the nerdy kids who were born sharp and grew up
honing that sharpness like a weapon
because they had no choice:
I see you.
I am you.
Never let the assholes dull your shine...
or your thorns.

CHAPTER ONE

POPPY, NOW

I HAVE a drawing that I keep tucked inside an old doll house—well, a house for fairies. My father always insisted upon the whimsical, albeit in small amounts. It's little quirks like that which make you real to people. Which make you safe. Everyone has some weird thing they cling to in times of stress, whether it's listening to a favorite song or snuggling up in a comfortable blanket or talking to the sky as if it might respond. I had the fairies.

And that little fairy house, now blackened by soot and flame, is as good a place as any to keep the things that should be gone. I haven't looked at the drawing since the day I brought it home, can't even remember stealing it, but I can describe every jagged line by heart.

The crude slashes of black that make up the stick figure's arms, the page torn where the scribbled lines meet—shredded by the pressure of the crayon's point. The sadness of the smallest figure. The horrific, monstrous smile on the father, dead center in the middle of the page.

Looking back, it should have been a warning—I should have known, I should have run. The child who drew it was no longer there to tell me what happened by the time I stumbled into that house. The boy knew too much, that was obvious from the picture.

Children have a way of knowing things that adults don't —a heightened sense of self-preservation that we slowly lose over time as we convince ourselves that the prickling along the backs of our necks is nothing to worry about. Children are too vulnerable not to be ruled by emotion—they're hard-wired to identify threats with razor's-edge precision. Unfortunately, they have a limited capacity to describe the perils they uncover. They can't explain why their teacher is scary or what makes them duck into the house if they see the neighbor peeking at them from behind the blinds. They cry. They wet their pants.

They draw pictures of monsters under the bed to process what they can't articulate.

Luckily, most children never find out that the monsters under their bed are real.

I never had that luxury. But even as a child, I was comforted that my father was a bigger, stronger monster than anything outside could ever be. He would protect me. I knew that to be a fact the way other people know the sky is blue or that their racist Uncle Earl is going to fuck up Thanksgiving. Monster or not, he was my world. And I adored him in the way only a daughter can.

I know that's strange to say—to love a man even if you see what terrors lurk beneath. My therapist says it's normal, but she's prone to sugarcoating. Or maybe she's so good at positive thinking that she's grown blind to real evil.

I'm not sure what she'd say about the drawing in the fairy house. I'm not sure what she'd think about me if I told her that I understood why my father did what he did, not because I thought it was justified, but because I understood him. I'm an expert when it comes to the motivation of the creatures underneath the bed.

And I guess that's why I live where I do, hidden in the New Hampshire wilderness as if I can keep every piece of the past beyond the border of the property—as if a fence might keep the lurking dark from creeping in through the cracks. And there are always cracks, no matter how hard you try to plug them. Humanity is a perilous condition rife with self-inflicted torment and psychological vulnerabilities, the what-ifs and maybes contained only by paper-thin flesh any inch of which is soft enough to puncture if your blade is sharp.

I knew that before I found the picture, of course, but something in those jagged lines of crayon drove it home, or dug it in a little deeper. Something changed that week in the mountains. Something foundational, perhaps the first glimmer of certainty that I'd one day need an escape plan. But though I like to think I was trying to save myself from day one, it's hard to tell through the haze of memory. There are always holes. Cracks.

I don't spend a lot of time reminiscing; I'm not especially nostalgic. I think I lost that little piece of myself first. But I'll never forget the way the sky roiled with electricity, the greenish tinge that threaded through the clouds and seemed to slide down my throat and into my lungs. I can feel the vibration in the air from the birds rising on frantically beating wings. The smell of damp earth and rotting pine will never leave me.

Yes, it was the storm that kept it memorable; it was the mountains.

It was the woman.

It was the blood.

CHAPTER TWO

POPPY, THEN

Night in the Alabama bayous encroaches with a decadence unknown in the bigger cities—harder and deeper. Like the rest of the world has been sucked into a void. The night it all started, the moon was hidden, too, the only light one low-hanging scarf of stars in the far east, which was not nearly enough to keep the shadows from wrapping around me like a blanket. The night breathed with me, a damp breeze redolent of sleeping magnolias. If my father had stopped the car right then, I'd have heard the tremulous *scree* of cicadas, the glumpy *blat-blat* of bullfrogs. As it was, only the buzzing drone of the tires against the highway filled my ears.

I adjusted myself in the seat, my face aimed at the truck's window, my blond curls springing against my cheek. I could smell the musty chill of ozone at the edge of the breeze. Even if the neighbors hadn't been talking about it all week, I would have known a storm was coming.

I glanced over at my father's bare face gleaming in the glare off the truck's instrument panel, his skin pasty, like pizza dough. I was nine years old, and I'd never seen him without his beard. He'd kept his mustache, though, perched on his upper lip like a curly brown caterpillar. I wondered if he'd ever been without the beard before, whether my mother had fallen in love with a clean-shaven man, if his cheeks were slick and pale the day she left us.

Dad seemed to feel me looking because he turned his head my way. "Are you excited, Poppy?"

We'd never been on vacation before, and the novelty of it prickled dully along my spine. "Of course I'm excited. Where are we going?"

My voice came out muffled—sleepy. He'd woken me at three in the morning with his keys already dangling from his fist. I didn't have time to register the kind of thrill that I probably should have felt, hadn't even asked where we were going, just climbed out of bed and followed him out to the truck.

He grinned, and with that bare, pale face, he felt like a mere impression of the man he usually was. Like I was driving off into the night with a stranger. "We're going to the mountains," he announced.

The... mountains? We weren't hikers. What would we do in the mountains? Had he rented a house to watch the wildlife? He often stared out from the back deck while the deer sniffed at his roses. But unlike everyone else in Alabama, my father would never shoot one; he said that guns were for cowards. It was wrong to blindside an animal that didn't see you coming, but more than that, there was no chase in it. What fun was the hunt if you couldn't see the fear in their eyes? At least, I assume that's what he might have thought. I don't have a personal frame of reference—I never liked hunting in any form, guns or not.

"I know what you're thinking," he went on. "What kind of fun can we have in the mountains? Right?"

I almost laughed—he had the uncanny ability to read my mind. But I could read him too, and that wasn't always comforting. Some things you didn't want to know.

"It'll be wonderful. You'll see."

"I know, Dad." And I did.

The miles of black highway stretched out forever, a hazy tunnel to a temporary freedom. No school, no pretending, no smiling while everyone else turned their backs on me. Just me and my dad and the mountains. Dad always said how important it was to be normal so as not to attract attention, but he attracted plenty of attention himself. He was the man who bought school supplies for the entire town. Who paid for the sheriff's department to get new equipment. He was as conspicuous in his heroism as I was in my solitude—I wasn't like the other kids, and it wasn't just my brains. I'm certain some of them knew exactly what my father was, but they couldn't put it into words. Their parents would never believe it anyway.

My father shifted lanes to pass a slower-moving sedan with a steady tick-tick-tick of his blinker, then hit the gas. "Go back to sleep, Poppy. I'll wake you when we get close."

I stretched my feet into the pocket in front of me. "Can we look for a waterfall?" I'd been assigned a report on waterfalls a few months before. I liked the thought that they'd take all your filth downstream instead of washing it down to be reabsorbed through the pads of your feet.

"I already looked up the perfect one. We'll be dancing in a waterfall soon enough."

I never even had to ask.

I relaxed back against the window and closed my eyes. The glass was hard and cool, bumping against my temple, but I liked the way it felt; it kept me on the verge of sleep without letting me drift away.

How strange that I still remember exactly how the window felt against my hair, how the leaked chill from the torn weather stripping smelled vaguely of exhaust. Yet I do not remember many things that others might deem important. My therapist says it's the trauma—that I couldn't remember if I wanted to. I think all of us have pieces of ourselves, of those we love, that we don't want to accept.

And though my father and I never once spoke of that week in the mountains after we went home, the memories of that time are a snapshot come to life while the rest of my childhood remains a puzzle that I never understood how to solve.

If there's one thing I know for sure, it's that thinking too hard about any of it only makes things worse.

CHAPTER THREE

THE SUN BEGAN to gray the horizon around five, illuminating a landscape pockmarked with hay bales and horses. The fruit Dad had packed did well for breakfast: two nectarines and a baggie of green grapes. He'd even brought me Squeeze-Its to drink, something he usually lamented about for having too much sugar. Just bringing it to my lips made my guts tighten up like I might be tempting a slow slide toward diabetes, and for what? They weren't even that good.

I dozed off and on throughout the later morning. I wished I had brought something with me—something to do. I'd barely had time to grab a single notebook so I could finish writing a letter to Johnny, my pen pal. Johnny was mostly dull, loved horses and sea turtles and Def Leppard. He even had sea turtles imprinted on the fancy stationery he sent me letters on every other week.

But Johnny was smart, which was what I had been hoping for when I snuck my name onto the older kids' pen pal list at school; with one K-12 for the entire town, I didn't even have to slip into another building. I simply said I was sixteen instead of nine so I could talk about books and philosophy and chemistry and whether I might like to be a writer one day. It's funny to think about that now, how the age of technology would have made this impossible—how every parent involved would probably have to talk over social media first, make sure someone else's delinquent kid wasn't going to be a bad influence from 500 miles away. It was a different time. Which was lucky, because I needed a place to put all those ideas so they didn't explode out of me in a way that would be suspicious. Any hint of above-average intelligence would make people pay attention. Safer to write it down and send it off to another state.

I snuggled down with my arms crossed and stared at the road. I didn't want to write to my pen pal in front of Dad—I hadn't even found a good time to tell him about Johnny yet. It had never seemed important enough to bring up. Or maybe Johnny was something that was just... mine.

The hay bales grew sparser until there were only trees and green, the hills brightening from gray to a hazy emerald that was all the more vibrant against the cloudy sky. Were we still in Alabama? The purple peaks in the distance seemed a lot bigger than the rolling green hills I was used to. Georgia, perhaps. Kentucky. Wildflowers lined the shoulders on either side of the highway, cobalt and pink and yellow and white, all dulled by the gauzy clouds. I hoped we could get to the waterfall before it started raining.

We drove for nine hours total, the truck's tires a steady drone like buzzing bees, the wind sweet in my hair.

I was drifting off again when the truck started ascending —I could feel it in my ears, the pressure that built and popped, and in the swaying of my body as he maneuvered the truck around hairpin curves. Higher. Higher. Finally, he slowed the truck to a crawl. I raised my head and blinked.

I had expected a campground, maybe a state park, but the landscape was mostly bare, with deeply rutted dirt, gouges like tiny canyons that made the truck rollick and whine. Where the street—more like a wide path—wasn't gouged, it was littered with reddish gravel, probably churned up when they cut the road through the mountain. The squat stumps of trees peppered the landscape for acres on either side, but the brush that bordered the road suggested that no one had been back here in some time. I could see the thicker woods in the distance, though, stately oaks, the spires of birches, the heavy girth of prickly pines that spread out like rolling waves and vanished into the cloud-shaded mountains. Perhaps this was once meant to be a neighborhood, cleared for townhomes before the market went bad. Or it might have been... an old logging road.

Either way, I did not believe that this was a place for hiking. Billy Bob and his tractor might find it fun, or the four-wheeler boys who thought mud was more thrilling than finding a job that didn't involve meth, but what kind of a vacation could we have amidst a field of hacked-off lumber?

I turned to my father, my brow furrowed in question.

Dad grinned back, a wide, bright-white smile—excited? Or pleased that I might be excited. I know now that the way he experienced the world was not the same as the way a normal person might, but making me happy was a goal in most any context. We crawled along the shoulder, my father edging off the road, the squeaking of the brakes almost obscured by the grinding crunch beneath the tires. Birds chirped in response, or perhaps in agitation.

And then... I saw it.

Outside my window, a tiny green ribbon fluttered in the breeze inches above the ground, thin and pale against the brown of the stump it was tied to. It was the kind of ribbon lumberjacks might use to alert others to a diseased plant, or to mark a birch that had to come down to make way for yet another cabin, but it was too clean to have been from the original demolition. New. Put there recently.

I straightened, my heart pounding. Dad used to set up treasure hunts for me, but I'd imagined the time for such games had passed. I was six the last time he'd woken me up early and sent me searching for a gift: fifteen clues to find the fairy house, all done up in sunny yellow with purple trim.

I grinned, staring at that ribbon. Was something hidden beneath the scrap of fabric, buried in the dirt? A tiny note, perhaps, a toy or a piece of carved metal to lead me to my next clue? Or would I find a clue gouged into the wood itself?

My father did not stop the car near the ribbon. He never made his treasure hunts easy—that would have been boring, and for a kid smart enough to blow through all the high school reading in elementary school, boring was insufferable.

I kept my gaze on the stump, *the clue*, while he slid the car along the shoulder for another hundred feet. I can hear the grinding noise of the gravel shoulder now, hushed but sharp as a blade. Funny the things you remember when you aren't trying.

The moment the truck stopped, I leaped out into the filmy afternoon, squinting. The crow on top of the stump made it easier to track—huge and black with shiny feathers and enormous charcoal eyes. With the harsh *thunk* of the slamming truck door still echoing in the breeze, I confidently headed off toward the dead tree. Birds sat on nearly every stump beyond the trunk I was watching, some so far off they resembled flakes of black pepper. Eerily quiet, not so much as a chitter from the birds. Not a rumble of thunder to break the stillness.

"Poppy?"

"Yeah?" I didn't turn. The green ribbon was still too far away to see, and I didn't want to mix up the crow atop that downed tree with a different one. I wanted to find the clue fast—to impress him.

"Come on back, Poppy."

Behind the bird, lightning flashed, brightening his inky feathers with a burst of silver as if we'd all been cast in a Hitchcock movie. "But I see the clue, Dad. I caught it on the way in." I sounded like I was whining—petulant. Pathetic. And I already knew from his tone that I had made an error. With a final fleeting glance at the trunk, I turned back to my father, disappointment burning in my chest.

He was frowning, the chalky light staining his skin, his gray T-shirt washing him out further—even his jeans were faded. Only his eyes were bright, a deep amber that glittered like the gaze of a tiger. "The clue?" He shook his head. "Sorry, no clues here. But I have something better. Something you don't have to search for."

I forced my face into a mask of calm acceptance, mostly angry at myself for being wrong. Sometimes a green ribbon attached to the trunk of an old, dead tree was just a ribbon, but when you were trained to watch for the smallest of details, it was easy to get confused. Easy to see clues where they did not exist.

My sneakers on the gravel made a grainy *cshh-cshh* sound as I walked back to the truck, my shoulders straight, my head held high. "Sorry, I thought I saw something. Can't be too careful, right, Dad?" *Nice save, dummy.* Even then, I knew that self-deprecation was a trick—something my dad used to make him more approachable in mixed company. I couldn't try it aloud, though. There weren't many things that upset my father, but hearing me insult myself might have been one of them.

I stopped beside him just as he pulled the latch on the truck's bed. *Clunk.* The birds exploded skyward with beating wings and strangely emphysemic screams.

"That's my smart Poppy. Always watching." He never did anything so trite as ruffling my hair, but that phrase felt like a pat on the back. He glanced at the sky, at the birds, then pulled his blade from his belt and sliced the ropes to release the tarp.

I stepped closer. *Huh.* Not just backpacks for our clothes—new sleeping bags, blue and black, were tied onto the top of each backpack. The backpacks themselves were new as well, mine bigger than the one I used at school, with thicker straps, presumably made for hiking. And... a tent? It hung in a bright orange oblong pouch off the side of the larger pack. *Interesting.* Mountains, yes, hiking sure, but sleeping out in the wilderness? My father wasn't the outdoorsy type, despite the acres of woods that surrounded our house in Alabama. He didn't fish. He didn't forage or take long walks in the woods. And he didn't hunt animals. How much food did he have in his pack?

As if in response to my thoughts, the sky growled, a long low rumble of thunder that vibrated my marrow. No, this was all wrong. Hadn't people in town been talking about a hurricane coming? This far north, there'd be no hurricane, of course, but storms like that always had far-reaching impacts. Tornadoes. Hail. Vicious stuff even hours from the coast.

Dad smiled, so strange without his beard, and slid the hunting knife that he had never once used for hunting back into the sheath beneath his shirt. He gestured to the smaller of the two packs. "Ready for an adventure?"

"I... think so." *Was* this a vacation? I think that was the first time I considered that it might be an exit plan—an escape. Change your face by shaving the most memorable part of you? *Check.* Pack a bag? *Check.* All that was left was to run away. I always thought we'd end up in a plane if we needed to leave Alabama, that we'd be somewhere over the ocean before the sheriff had a chance to arrest him. Maybe no one would find us if we lived off the land forever—which I couldn't imagine—but someone would find his truck if he left it here.

I raised my gaze to the sky, to those pregnant clouds. Darker now, for sure.

My father already had his own pack on his shoulders, no challenge for him as strong as he was—well-defined biceps that didn't even ripple with the weight of the bag. He pulled my pack from the truck bed and held it up so I could slip my arms through the straps. Heavy—quite heavy. And sitting on the zipper...

I gasped and stumbled backward as the roach skittered onto my arm, then dropped to the ground.

My father's laughter roared through the trees. I squinted at the dirt, at the roach unmoving near my left shoe—the insect was fake. Or... maybe dead. I didn't know which, and it didn't matter. What mattered was that he'd put it there.

My shoulders relaxed, though my heart was still lodged in my throat. "Dad!" But his laughter was contagious. I laughed with him—I couldn't help it. But I still didn't like the way the roach was crouched there, as if it might spring back to life and attack me. I lifted my foot over the thing, still giggling. My father raised an eyebrow—

no longer laughing. I lowered my foot, leaving the insect uncrushed.

He nodded and turned his head to the field, the tree graveyard smoky with mist. "Come on, Poppy. Let's go."

"Do you think it will rain?"

"If it does, we have shelter. But I'm not afraid." That much was always true—fear was not one of the emotions my father experienced. "Are you afraid, my sweet Poppy? I like to think a girl like you isn't scared of anything." *Not even roaches.* He didn't say the last part aloud, but I heard it all the same.

I squared my shoulders, the straps already digging into the soft spots on either side of my neck. "Of course I'm not afraid." But the truth was, I didn't know. It would take me years to truly understand fear—in others and in myself. Even if I'd been trembling inside, I would have smiled, but as it was, all I felt was a little sick. From the Squeeze-Its, I was sure.

"Good. It would be silly for you to be scared. You're stronger than anything out there." He slammed the truck's hatch and adjusted the straps on his backpack, then headed off along the gravel, a single shadowed figure framed by the far-off trees, the field of stumps spread out on either side like corpses on a battlefield. The air was damp inside my nostrils, fingers of breeze tugging at my shirt, pushing me forward after him. Even now I can still see him if I squint into a cloudy day at just the right angle, the square lines of his shoulders, his hips rolling confidently. The way his stocky silhouette seemed to get bigger as he walked away from me.

CHAPTER FOUR

THESE WERE THE QUIET MOMENTS. They were the times I clung to later, the moments that kept him real for me. Even after he was arrested, when public opinion shifted from hero to maniac, I saw him the way he was in those mountains.

Before it all went wrong.

Dad had packed leftover barbecue in plastic sandwich bags. I can smell the chicken now, the tang of vinegar that wafted from his lips and caught my nose as I trudged along behind him. It would have tasted like sugar on the tongue, molasses and cheap chili peppers. I chewed stalks of celery instead, snarfed up cornbread muffins that our neighbor Millie brought him. I never liked barbecue, only choked it down when the locals gave me trouble in their typical "just a little, oh bless your heart" kind of way. My father would have been disappointed if he knew that—*it's not your job to make yourself uncomfortable for them, Poppy*—but I knew he wanted us to blend in. Couldn't do that without eating meat, not in southern Alabama where barbecue was more a religion than anything that was found in a church. I didn't need to get the gossips started on the rude weird girl who'd hurt the reverend's feelings at the church potluck.

Gossip has always been the lifeblood of small towns, chatter devoid of compassion, a giddy exhilaration at someone else's struggles. If they'd looked a little closer, they might've noticed that my father's eyes never lit up when he smiled. Not unless he was looking my way. But they only ever saw what they wanted to see.

"You okay, Poppy?"

I wiped a hand over my brow; my fingers came away damp. The air had an edge to it, but the traveling clouds had sucked up that damp gulf coast breeze, the heavy wetness of swamp. Blades of sunlight sliced through the cloud cover now and then, bathing my sneakers in dappled gold. "I'm fine, Dad."

And I was. Yes, if the gossips knew everything, my father would have been behind bars and not raising a child, but he was better to me than any of the locals were to their kids. While my classmates couldn't sit right because their parents beat them bloody over a curse word, my father was teaching me to steer clear of any man who raised a hand in anger. To this day, I would never accept even a glancing blow from someone whom I cared about.

That's not what love looks like.

I shifted the pack; I was sweating beneath the straps. "Where's the waterfall?"

"It'll take a few more hours to get there. We might not make it until tomorrow."

Tomorrow? *How long will we be hiking?* But it never occurred to me to ask him. It would take as long as it took.

I trudged on. My upper back ached after a while, but the air was cool enough to dry the sweat and kept my armpits from feeling sticky. The clouds had thickened, tinged with an unearthly green that made the sky feel watchful. And the woods themselves... they were *alive*.

The forest rustled with squirrels and other unseen creatures, the frantic skittering of claws in underbrush. The leaves shuddered with pre-storm energy. Even the trees were more vibrant than usual in the filtered gloom.

Soon, the mountains grew steeper, the cliffs slicing down into gorges thick with jagged boulders and spindly pines; my thighs burned. Sometimes Dad would hurry ahead, and I picked my way through brambles and dewberry, trying to keep up. When we found ourselves on any semblance of a path, I ran, the pack bouncing against the small of my back and clacking my teeth together. I was young, not in bad shape, but my short legs were no match for my father's stride.

The sky grew darker as afternoon waned into evening, the thunder rumbling on and off, but there was no rain yet. Just the whisper of it, a promise that soon the skies would open and turn the world into a hazy blur of violent water. The path had thinned again. Dad and I walked single file along sheer cliffs—not so much as a branch to break a fall. But my father kept smiling, so I did not panic. I wouldn't go over the side. He wouldn't let me get hurt. He'd die first.

I breathed the humid air into my lungs and let it massage my insides. It always made me feel powerful, standing outside with the electric wind swirling around me, like the thunderclouds were responding to every twitch of my hand, hearing what was in my heart.

"I think this is it." Dad had stopped and turned back to me, his bare face shiny with sweat, the new skin on his chin pink like a baby's.

I looked around. The slender path was scarce, the dirt marred by snared picker vines and fallen leaves. On my left, so close I could touch the rock, mountains ascended into the clouds, the gray stone run through with bands of white that shone like a river to the sky. Ten feet or so to my right, the cliff dropped off. I squinted over the precipice where plants clung to the crevices in the sheer wall, as if terrified they might plummet to the rocks below. I couldn't see the bottom, but I could imagine the jagged spikes of stone waiting to shatter them. Shatter me.

Dad hauled his backpack off and set it against the rock face. "Here, we'll be well-protected on all sides. And there's space to make a fire."

Well-protected? I frowned at the ledge—the cliff.

He leveled his gaze at me. "We won't fall, Poppy. We can put up barriers if that will make you more comfortable —stones to block off the cliff overnight. But we'll just be sleeping inside the tent, and you're certainly not prone to sleepwalking." He winked, then knelt beside his bag and went to work opening the orange pouch.

I shifted toward the wall of rock and dropped my own pack at my feet. "You're really good at this, Dad."

"I'm only as good as my hiking partner." He chuckled.

But my eyes weren't on him. A butterfly had landed on my bag, its yellow and black wings pulsing in a lackadaisical way, like it had just boarded a bus and was settling in for the ride. Fairies and butterflies felt remarkably similar—it was in the way a butterfly remade its entire body out of goo. The way a fairy could hide behind a flower stem but chose to flit about her forest haven, predators be damned. It was all a little magical. All a little brave.

I reached toward the bag, wanting to be closer to it, but the butterfly flapped its wings, then skittered haphazardly along the brush at the cliff's edge before diving into the gorge.

I sighed.

"Sometimes you have to let them go, Poppy."

I dragged my gaze from the spot where the insect had vanished. "Who do I have to let go?"

My father was sitting on his knees, turned fully sideways. He held the tent pole half built in his hand, sticking from his fist like a riding crop. "Butterflies. Too much pressure and they crack. The same goes for people."

Ah, of course. He was always trying to impart some life lesson or another—all dads probably did that, though perhaps in less obscure ways. I thought I knew what he meant, though. My mom had cracked—she'd left soon after I was born. A child was too much pressure for her. But we couldn't have done anything to make her stay; you couldn't force love, or more to the point, loyalty.

He jammed the pole into the dirt, his face hidden by the bulk of his shoulder. His muscles rippled beneath his T-shirt as he secured the skinny tubes. "It's okay to have a temporary friend, though—someone fun to meet a need, but that you don't necessarily trust all the way." He glanced over his shoulder and met my eyes. "I figured that's what your pen pal was all about."

The breeze went cold. I opened my mouth, but I couldn't speak—all that escaped was a shaky hiss of air. I wasn't worried about him being mad; he was never angry at me. But the fact that he knew... *How did he know?*

He dragged one corner of his mouth into a grin. "You look surprised."

"I didn't want to bother you with it, Dad." I dropped my gaze to the backpack—to the spot where the butterfly had briefly perched. "It's not like we're friends. Those letters are just a place where I can talk about things that interest me."

He nodded, just once. "My smart girl. I'm proud of you

—you knew what you needed, and you took it, rules be damned. But the school wouldn't assign you a pen pal without me knowing."

Ah. I hung my head. Other kids had pen pals, too, and I think there was even a permission slip, now that he mentioned it. I'd just never brought it home. But of course the teacher would have handed it to him in person. He could have chosen who I was assigned to if he wanted. He didn't though; he wouldn't have chosen a boy.

In the sickly light of the evening, his bare face had taken on a ghoulish tinge—too pale, too yellow-green to be healthy. "Better for me to know. What do you think I would have done if I had found out that some stranger was writing you?"

My blood froze. "I don't know, Dad." But I did. "Maybe you'd have sent him a dictionary so he could keep up with me."

He laughed this time, a boisterous sound that rattled the tent poles and shook the leaves. It probably wasn't that intense, but memory highlights certain things that might not be entirely accurate. "Perhaps I'll do that when we get home," he said. "I'm sure that boy needs help. You're wicked sharp."

Wicked sharp. It's something you might say in Boston—I know that now after living in New Hampshire. Back then, the phrase just felt out of place, a piece of him that made him special.

I wonder sometimes if he was raised somewhere else. Maybe if I poke around, I'll find a trail of unsolved crimes that leads from one corner of the country to the other, finally ending in Alabama where the cost of living was so low that it hardly took anything for him to be the biggest benefactor in the town. Criminals need a community of people unwilling to believe what they are if the truth ever comes out. He wanted to fit in, to be one of them, but just a cut above—relatable yet so helpful and pious that if he were ever caught, he'd have a world ready to defend him.

And that's exactly what happened.

CHAPTER FIVE

We dug a hole for the fire pit, scraping at the earth until my fingers hit the stone beneath. I collected rocks to make a border so the fire couldn't spread; he collected the twigs and a few larger logs which we stacked in a triangle in the center.

No hot dogs for us, though. My father knew that I would not eat smoke-infused burgers or blackened marshmallows. Instead, he'd brought Lunchables, another thing he never purchased at home—*too much salt, not good for your heart, sweet girl.* I waited for him to pull out a different meal for himself, perhaps a sandwich or more chicken, but he produced his own Lunchable and peeled off the top —pizza.

We ate by firelight, orange and gold flickering against the stripes on my athletic pants like my legs were on fire. The leaves on the kindling curled and blistered and burned loose from their moors to skitter around our heads—little fireflies of death should they catch the right tree. But they didn't.

The night stretched into oblivion, the woods inky black

to match the sky. The silence stretched, too, giving voice to those creatures that called the woods home. We located a place to use the bathroom down the path, far enough from the tent to avoid unfortunate smells, but the walk back felt treacherous enough that I made up my mind to wait until morning. When the lightning started, we ducked inside the tent and snuggled down inside our sleeping bags. There's a storm in Alabama nearly every week during hurricane season, but no matter how the wind howled, how raucous the world became outside those windows, my father always kept the inside of our home calm. He was never one to be riled up.

The ground beneath the tent was stone, like trying to fall asleep on a bathroom floor. The bed of pine needles we'd spread over the rocky ground did little to ease the pressure on my joints. Everything from the tent to the sleeping bags gave off the chemical stink of plastic—new vinyl—and my father's gentle snores drowned out the birds and the crickets, even the breeze, more violent with each passing hour. But it didn't matter. My elbow was the last thing I registered in my visual field, sticking out into the middle of the tent, traversing the gap between my sleeping bag and my sleeping father like a pale, skinny bridge.

When I next opened my eyes, my elbow was tucked up under my head. Rain attacked the tent's roof, but the woods were louder still, the insects buzzing in the frenzied way of wild places. My neck ached from the way I had twisted myself up to keep my face off the ground.

I wriggled deeper inside the sleeping bag—too hot for the sultry weather—and tried to close my eyes against the murky blackness of the tent. *Something's wrong*. It wasn't the storm—the slap and patter of rain was easy to pick out of the din, an agitated *pit-tap-pit-pit*. No, it was the bugs that weren't quite... right. The cicadas were too loud, too harsh, and not quite constant enough for the natural ebb and flow of a calling swarm.

I pushed myself to seated, blinking in the dark. I didn't need the flashlight to know I was alone. The sleeping bag beside me was crumpled and cold.

Where was my father?

The droning buzzing came again, whining and high-pitched, though far enough off that I had to strain my ears. Not bugs for sure, and not an animal—no animal made a sound like that. It ceased as quickly as it had started, yet I could still hear the echo against the walls of the tent. Electric, almost. But that was impossible.

I carefully pulled my legs from the sleeping bag, stuffed my feet into my sneakers, and clambered toward the exit, squinting, trying to force my eyes to adjust.

The rain hit me the moment I poked my head from the tent, pricking at my arms like needles. Outside the tent, the sound was clearer, though still distant, a mile or two off, perhaps a little farther with the way sound carried out here. A definitely mechanical whirring that vibrated the tiny bones in my eardrums and set my teeth on edge.

A... chainsaw? Yes, a chainsaw. Somewhere back the way we'd come. But the logging area where we'd entered was half a day's hike from here, and no one would be out working in the middle of the night, especially not in a storm. The only people here were me and my father, and we hadn't carried a gas-powered chainsaw up from the car, I was positive on that front.

"Dad?" I pushed myself to my feet just outside the tent, raising my hand like a visor against the rain, but it did no good. The woods outside the tent were black, black, black, any moonlight choked out by the pregnant clouds. The buzzing ceased.

"Dad!" I called again. He had to be nearby—perhaps he'd heard the chainsaw and gone to investigate.

Water dripped in slick, cold rivulets down my face and off my scalp, soaking the back of my neck. I could feel my way along the rock, but I wasn't willing to go far, not so near the cliff's edge. I was no match for a hundred-foot drop onto a bed of jagged stone.

Still, I could see a hazy lightness along the horizon—six o'clock maybe. I'd be able to see better within fifteen or twenty minutes. I should go back inside the tent. I could ask my dad about the chainsaw when he returned.

If he returned.

My chest tightened. What if my father went to see who was working out there and fell down the mountain? It was dark, and the rocks were slippery with rain. But he wouldn't go off hiking for miles in the middle of the night and leave me here alone.

"Dad! Dad, can you hear me?" But the moment the words were in the air, it felt like a mistake. Gooseflesh shivered up my arms. My lungs were soggy with humidity. I reached out, searching for the rock wall—I'd just keep my hand on the stone and go very slowly. Very carefully.

I eased forward. I felt foggy, discombobulated, as if I were stepping into an alien landscape where my father no longer existed, where no one else existed except for me and whoever was wielding that chainsaw in the middle of a storm like a maniac. I just wanted to hear my father's voice. I needed to know he was okay.

Wind plastered my curls against the side of my face, the *tap-tap-pit-tap-pit* of the rain accelerating, not that it mattered—I was already soaked to the bone. I shuddered, then took another cautious step, my hand still out, seeking the stone wall. I touched only air.

The buzzing drone came back, a far-off grinding—a burst of metal against wood. I edged forward again, uncertainty wrapping my throat in a viselike grip. *Someone else is out here, someone—*

And then I was flying through the air, my arms pinwheeling, *oh god, falling, I'm falling off the mountain!* A scream rose in my throat. I landed hard on my chest, the air exploded from my lungs, and a sharp stabbing lanced through my ribs. But that pain was nothing compared to my leg. Agony erupted up through my heel and spread, burning, to my knee. There was relief, too, that I wasn't plummeting through open space to my death, but my leg, my leg, *my leg.*

I rolled onto my side, whimpering. But only part of me rolled—my ankle was stuck fast.

That's when I screamed.

I tried to pull my leg closer to my body, but the pain was awful, shooting and jagged and hot. As if on cue, lightning sparked across the heavens. My foot remained stuck—*what am I caught on?*

I cried out—"Dad! Help!"—but the weak syllables were lost in another burst of chainsaw buzzing, then a deafening clap of thunder. In the brilliant white light that followed, I could see my shoe—tangled in vines? No... vines weren't white, and what I saw in that flash of lightning was not prickly dewberry or a nest of kudzu. A rope? Maybe if it was extremely thin. I fingered the tie—it sure felt like a thin rope—but just wiggling it sent bursts of white-hot agony sizzling up through my hip. Without the lightning, I couldn't see—could not see my foot, could not see into the savage murk of the raging storm.

The hairs rose along the back of my neck.

I turned my head, peering into the trees that separated me from the cliff—nothing but blackness. I looked back down the path, but it was too dark to make out anyone lurking among the stones. But eyes... they were boring into my flesh. Someone was watching me, I was sure—or *something*. A bear? A wolf? Either made more sense than a person. Some kind of apex predator, just waiting in the woods until I turned my back.

I was prey.

I was *trapped*.

I gingerly tugged at the knots around my foot, but only tightened the tie. I moaned, gritting my teeth, and tugged harder, my shoe grinding against my ankle like sandpaper, but I didn't only feel it on my flesh—I felt it inside the bone, stabbing my marrow, shards of broken glass in my veins.

Trapped, my brain screamed again; I was trapped and alone, and I couldn't see, and since my father wouldn't leave me to fend for myself as long as he drew breath... was he already dead? I was not a child who swore often, but the words that ripped themselves loose in the moments that followed would have made a trucker blush. And I shrieked every single one at the top of my lungs.

But no creature emerged from the woods to devour me.

No one came to save me.

The chainsaw buzzed on.

Lighting zapped across the sky. Pain tore from my ankle to my thigh, up my spine, and into my brain where it exploded into a thousand white-hot stars.

I ground my teeth against the pain—against the lightning in my blood.

Then there was only blackness.

CHAPTER SIX

Dawn comes fast in the wilderness. When my eyes finally blinked open, squinting through the raindrops at the leafy canopy above, the sky was the dark greenish gray of stormy twilight. I hadn't been lying there for long—ten or fifteen minutes on the outside—but it felt like an eternity. The rain splattered against my face, like being spit on by a passive-aggressive deity.

I turned my head. My neck ached as if each tendon was stretched over razor wire, but my ankle hurt worse, a steady, hideous throbbing. I could not see my father on the path. *He's gone over the side.* He had to have gone over the side. I was alone and injured in the middle of the mountains, probably being stalked by predators based on the incessant rustling in the brush, too heavy and deliberate to be the rain.

I managed to push myself to seated and winced at the ground—at my foot. *Wait.* I was... free? No rope twisted my ankle in its gnarled grasp, only the pale gray stones, several of them pushed in tight together; so tight it would have been easy to catch my foot in the stones themselves if

I'd stepped the wrong way. Had I imagined the rope? I was sure I'd felt it, but what other explanations were there?

I sniffed and clenched my jaw to stop my teeth from chattering. I'd think better once I wasn't in so much pain, but I couldn't just sit here while I healed. My skin was greenish and mottled beneath the hem of my tattered athletic pants. My toes were numb, too, the shoe too tight—my foot was swelling. No, I couldn't walk out of here. And the rain was still a steady drizzle seeping straight into my blood. But there were sleeping bags in the tent. My backpack with spare clothes. I could get dried off, then figure out a plan.

The bushes rustled again—closer, definitely closer. My shoulders tightened, and I jerked toward the sound in time to see a figure emerge from around the side of the rock wall, something white and puffy clutched in his hand. *Dad!* My heart leaped, but I was still clenching my jaw with pain and cold. I probably looked angry that he was there.

He stopped short when he saw me on the ground, then rushed toward me—too fast, much too fast so close to the cliff—but I found I couldn't care. I'd never been more relieved to see him.

He tossed his package on the dirt and dropped to his knees beside me, eyebrows knitted. "What are you doing out of the tent... on the ground? What happened?"

"I... I fell." I wasn't especially prone to emotional outbursts—it was the pain that made my voice quaver the way it did then, or maybe the weather. I trembled in my drenched clothes. "Where were you?"

"How'd you fall?" he went on as if he hadn't heard my question, reaching for my foot. "And why didn't you go inside after?"

"I tripped on a rope. I was all tangled up, and I couldn't get it off, and..."

He frowned. I followed his gaze to the stones—bare stones, no rope. Just my busted foot, the ankle bone encased in a swollen baseball of flesh. "A... rope? Was it maybe your shoelace?" He gestured to a spot beneath the bottom of my shoe, an angle I couldn't see from my vantage point.

I craned my neck to peer around the sole of my sneaker —*oh*. I hadn't tied my shoes in my haste to get out of the tent. Now I noticed that hidden behind my heel, the white laces from my left shoe were jammed down between two stones, tethering me to the spot more with pain than with substance. Of course. *Way to go, dummy*.

My father shifted the rocks, freeing the lace. "Come here, Poppy. Let me help you."

I reached for him, forcing myself not to moan when I shifted my foot from its spot on the rocks—trying not to puke. Had Dad packed Tylenol?

He slipped an arm around me and lifted me onto my good foot. I clung to him, wincing, matching his movements until I was vertical, then said: "Did you hear the chainsaw?"

The rain on his bare face made him look older, or maybe it was the lines around his mouth that weren't visible when he had the beard. "The... chainsaw?"

"Just a few minutes ago. Someone was working out there, a few miles back the way we came. I thought maybe you went to see what they were doing."

He raised an eyebrow. "I just went to use the bathroom. Dinner didn't agree with me, and it seemed... considerate to walk a bit farther from the tent." He nodded to a roll of toilet paper encased in a large plastic freezer bag—the puffy white item he'd been carrying. "But I was only gone ten minutes, maybe fifteen. I came back and found you on the rocks."

I frowned. "I came out to see what was going on." My stomach was sour too—the Lunchables. And that chainsaw had been faint, farther away than a ten-minute hike. Even if he'd left me here while he investigated—which he would not have done—there was no way he'd have made it back here to find me on the stones so quickly. The distance alone certainly made it possible that he hadn't heard it.

But I wasn't crazy. I wouldn't have come out of the tent for nothing. "Dad, I swear I heard—"

He shifted his arm, and I leaned harder against him, my fingers slipping against his rain-slicked bicep. "I believe you," he said. "I don't need convincing. If you say you heard a chainsaw, you heard it. It's just that I *didn't* hear it. Is it possible that you were dreaming?"

Maybe? I thought I'd seen a rope too. Thought I'd heard a bear in the woods. And bears didn't come out of the woods to attack people—they wanted nothing to do with us. Heck, I rarely wanted anything to do with humans, and I was one.

He was still watching me, rainwater dripping down his cheeks, eyebrows raised like he was concerned, but I didn't think it was concern. I studied his face, the tight corners of his lips, the way the lower lid of his eyes was pulled *just so* toward his temples—*he's disappointed.*

My chest heated despite the chill in the air. "I'm sure you're right. Why would anyone use a chainsaw in the middle of the night? It makes no sense." Water dripped into my mouth, spluttered from my lips when I spoke.

He smiled, more satisfied than happy. "And despite it not making sense, still you came out of that tent looking for me. You're fearless."

I was always fearless. There was no room to be scared,

not in a house like ours. "Thanks, Dad."

"You've got me—I'll take care of you." His eyes bored into mine. "You trust me, don't you?"

I nodded, though it sent a fresh spike of pain through my neck. "I know, Dad. And I do." The banter was helping, I realized. So was standing still.

He finally released my gaze and turned his face toward the cliffs. "Can you walk?"

I wanted to say yes, god I did. I wanted to be strong and responsible. But then I leaned away from him and lowered my foot, slowly, slowly—

I made a sound that was half hiss and half moan, and I hated myself for that. But I couldn't help it. The pain was exquisite—electric.

"It might be broken," he said, tugging me against him once more. Even in the dim light, the flesh around my ankle bone was darker than it had been. Purple and green, mottled like a dead man. Like it *was* already dying. Maybe my foot would rot clean off before we could get to a hospital.

The thunder rolled again; lightning crackled across the sky. The wind gusted jagged-glass rain onto my flesh and every shard that pierced the skin of my ankle shot through me like a dart.

Dad moved again, bending down, jolting my leg in a way that made me gasp as he threaded his forearm beneath my knees and lifted me into his arms. "We need to get out of here."

I needed a dry pair of pants—a warm shirt. "But it's cold, and all our stuff—"

"None of it matters." He started off over the path, the cliff dropping to oblivion on our left, the stones high and mighty on our right. "All that matters is you."

CHAPTER SEVEN

I CLUNG TO MY FATHER, nestling into the heat of his chest for comfort. I ground my teeth together, half from the agony that brightened in my ankle every time he took a step, and half to keep them from chattering—it made me feel weak.

"Don't worry, Poppy. I'll make sure you get to see another waterfall."

My fingers were claws on his shoulders. I wasn't worried about the waterfall. "Okay."

Within five minutes, the rain had intensified, sheeting down around us and making the terrain slicker. It hid the path, too—I could barely make out Dad's sneakers against the sloppy dirt. "Are we going to walk all the way back to the truck?"

"I'll find a place to take shelter. We need help."

Oh no. This was bad—really bad. My father never asked for help, and for him to say that now... he thought I was in bad shape. But we were in the middle of the mountains, half a day from our truck with not so much as a cleared hunting trail before us. And the cliffs seemed even more treacherous through the fog of rain—I could no longer see the brambles clinging to the side, making whatever lurked below more dangerous and sinister.

He stumbled, and I gripped him harder, but he righted himself quickly. And kept walking.

"I can wait a day, Dad. We can go back to the campsite and wait in the tent for the storm to pass. It's just a sore ankle." It wasn't *just* a sore ankle, but what good were two working ankles if we slid over a cliff? It was like bragging about your cholesterol before being thrown out of a plane, or refusing to eat cake before a lethal injection.

He shook his head. "I need to get you to a hospital. I didn't pack any painkillers, and I won't let you suffer all day."

"But what if we make a wrong turn? What if there's nothing out here?"

"I know from the maps that there are clearings due north—a highway thirty miles or so beyond where we made camp. There should be a house or two."

And so it went. Rain pelted us, my ankle throbbed, and every question I had was met with a reason why we should keep going. A few hours, that was all. A few miles more, and we'd be safe. I could make it. *I can make it.*

Thunder growled and growled and growled, a predator stalking us from the sky. My father walked quickly, faster than I would have dared over the rain-soaked path. I screwed my eyes closed and focused on the steady throbbing of his heart.

I'm not sure how long it had been, but he stopped walking so suddenly that for a split second, I was convinced he'd seen the bear I had felt in the woods, its claws poised and ready to tear us limb from limb. I raised my head, pulling myself up against his shoulder. The rain poured down in earnest here; the mossy-gray sky above us was unmarred by trees, the grass flushed a sickly green. A clearing—we had made it to a clearing. And...

Whoa.

The enormous log cabin was tucked right against the side of the mountain, the cliff's face pale blue beyond it like the backdrop of a school photo. Wooden beams the color of honey framed the front porch and stood vigil around every window—a piney exoskeleton. Along the left side, I could make out the exposed brick of what might have been a fireplace if not for the odd egg-like shape. A stone oven? My father said those made good pizzas. Beyond the rounded stone outcropping, a wrought iron fence with a simple latch surrounded a kidney-shaped pool, the water reflecting the green-tinged clouds.

My father started across the marshy lawn.

There was something else back there, too, another building behind the main house. Maybe a pool house, or a garage from the narrow fork of driveway that led back around the pool. Asphalt snaked from the front door to the tree line where it made a sudden steep descent toward what must be the main road. But the road itself was hidden in the fog beyond the hills. And when I closed my eyes and listened, there were no highway noises; even in the rain, I should have been able to hear the occasional blare of a truck's horn. Whoever lived here was about as far from humanity as they could get. But they probably had a car and might brave the storm to take us to the emergency room, even if it was a long drive.

The front door was darker than the honeyed beams, painted in a reddish stain that matched the flowerpots on either corner of the front porch, full-grown ficus trees bracing themselves against the wind. Sprigs of ivy lay flattened on the porch, their heart-shaped leaves torn from the vines.

"Do you think anyone's home?" I asked. Lights twinkled through the enormous bay windows that fronted the house, but those lights also illuminated the world inside—no movement. No people.

"They're home." He shifted me in his arms as if he might set me down to knock. I raised my fist instead, but as I lowered it toward the jamb, the reddish door moved away from me, hissing open on well-oiled hinges.

The woman on the other side was skinny through the arms with long thin fingers, but curvy through the chest and backside. My father always said that real women came in variations of health. And she had that healthy, wholesome kind of look about her, what I always called a "vanilla mom" look—the kind of mom who made sugar cookies in high heels just because she could. Most moms in Riverside were plain and boring and just... there. But not this woman. Her perfectly brushed light-brown hair was streaked with shades of goldenrod. Even her makeup was perfect despite being home in the middle of a storm: navy eyeliner, subtle brown mascara, shimmery gloss on her lips, muted bronzed blush on her cheekbones. She was the kind of woman who'd have gauze—who'd have Tylenol and ice.

"Oh my word!" she said. She laid a hand over her chest, nails cut short but perfectly manicured in translucent coral polish like she wanted people to believe they were natural.

I almost laughed at how perfectly fitting the expression was for a woman like that. I was weirdly giddy, light with endorphins. Relief, maybe, at having shelter. Or the pain—pain made people act weird too.

"Ma'am, I am so sorry to be botherin' you like this, but we got caught up out in the storm. My daughter tried to climb a waterfall, and the drizzle made the stones around it way too slick." That deep-southern accent coming out of my father's mouth always made the hairs on my neck stand up —far heavier than his normal accent. But pretending you're one of them was the easiest way to make people think you weren't a threat. In the south, a northern accent on the nicest of people would get side eye. I always figured they were still mad over "the war of Northern aggression" based on the way they flew those Confederate flags. My father said being a sore loser just meant you're weak-minded, unable to accept your failures. I'm still inclined to believe him.

"Oh, you poor dear," she said. I could see her bringing a tray of cookies to a group of shiftless children, a wide Vanna White smile brightening her features, crinkling the corners of her eyes. Telling them that dinner would be ready at six. She waved us inside. "You come right in before you catch your death."

"Much obliged, ma'am." Dad stepped carefully over the threshold and onto the front mat, which was no match for our dripping clothes. A puddle formed almost immediately around my father's shoes. But she was prepared like any vanilla mom should be—a blanket from the couch. She wrapped it over my father's shoulders and tucked it around my forearm.

"Leave your shoes here, and I'll get you some dry clothes. Sound good?" She smiled, head cocked like she wanted an answer, but why would anyone choose to sit in cold wet clothes? I was shivering again by then, the kiss of air conditioning raising gooseflesh on my arms and legs.

My father nodded. "Thanks much. But if we can use your phone to call an ambulance, we'll be on our way."

The smile on her pretty face fell. "Oh dear. That will be

a problem. The storm is doing a number on us—knocked the phone lines out. I have no idea when they'll be back up running, but it might be days, maybe longer." She gestured to the bay windows, the wind whipping greenery against the glass. "The mountains, you know? It's lovely, but phone service isn't the best. Keeps most people closer to the cities."

It's funny to think about that moment now. Fifteen years later, and Dad would have had a cell phone and no need for a landline—no reason to trudge through the woods in search of a house, no excuse to knock on her door. But he might have found one anyway.

CHAPTER EIGHT

So there we were, dripping onto some rich woman's floor, probably ruining her hardwoods while she looked on with concern written in the fine lines around her mouth.

We had no phone, which meant no ambulance. And I sure didn't see any neighbors. But if they had a car... they had to, right? Just because I hadn't seen one yet didn't mean it wasn't there.

My father edged me toward the couch, following the woman who introduced herself as "Sherry, like the drink, but with a C-H." New Orleans was only a few hours from our house in Alabama, and Dad and I visited a day or two each summer, so I'd always heard "Cherie" as a term of endearment: *Here are your beignets, cherie. Ya'll headed for the French Quarter, cherie?* But in New Orleans, people said it through a thick Cajun accent, a hard-to-understand dialect that accentuated unexpected syllables and muffled hard-edged consonants, turning anything they said into poetry. Cherie sounded like she was from... Minnesota? Michigan?

But she had kind eyes, and her fingertips on my arm

were gentle—consoling. My father lowered me onto the chocolate-colored couch, supple, like butter, and somehow warmer than my skin. Cherie winced when my foot hit the arm and hissed an inhale with me when I squeaked out a little cry. Very empathetic, perhaps overly so. Were most moms like that? I didn't have the experience to know for sure.

"Are you okay, Poppy?" my father asked.

I nodded. "I'm okay. It just... it hurts." I wished that it didn't. The burning behind my eyelids felt wrong—a pointless overreaction. I'd never seen my father cry, either.

I straightened up as best I could against the leather, trying to distract myself from the throbbing. The enormous room was separated into zones by distinctive seating. Here, two long leather couches flanked by wooden end tables sat atop an oriental rug. The end tables featured ornately carved vines, the same vines I'd seen in the potted plant on the porch, an attention to detail only the very wealthy could afford. Across the expanse of dark hardwood were four chairs positioned around a stone table that might have been marble. A grand piano occupied the far-right corner behind the marble table, an archway to the front side of it, beyond which was presumably the kitchen. The entire front wall was stonework, stacked river rocks with an opening in the middle for a fireplace, the hearth flanked by vases taller than I was. But the fireplace was not in the right location for that egg-shaped brickwork I'd seen from the outside.

My father looked on without comment, though I could hear what he was thinking: *What a waste of cash.* Money was for goodwill, a commodity critical to survival. Fancy vases just showed the world how much money you had—how special you were. It was bragging. And it made most people hate you more than they'd admit.

Cherie adjusted a pillow beneath my ankle, and I coughed to cover a moan.

She lowered herself to the floor beside the couch. "May I?" She held up her hands. I nodded—I didn't think she could do more damage. Her fingertips were feather light as she carefully palpated my leg from the knee to the shin over my athletic pants, then the bruised flesh below the hem. I took deep breaths, trying to ignore the needle-sharp sensations when she got closer to my ankle. The honey color at the crown of her head shimmered in the low light—her hair matched the outside of the house, I realized. Everything warm and sweet as honey. She frowned at my foot—the swelling, the bruising. "Oh sweetheart, I'm so sorry you're hurtin'. When my husband gets back, he can drive you to your car, or out to the emergency room." She raised her gaze to my father, who stood near my head, drying his hair with the blanket she'd wrapped around us. "Where did you park?"

My father opened his mouth to answer, but he never got that far.

A bang sounded from the back of the house, through the arch—the kitchen? Had to be. The entrance to the pool had to be that way too. Smart, really, to have the kitchen by the pool—snacks on the water, the epitome of luxury. It seemed like a very rich-person thing to do.

But the man who stomped in through that archway did not appear rich. If Cherie was a vanilla mom, the man who entered was an angry-skinhead type in a raincoat that matched the gray stones. Milk-pale skin, buzzed hair, black stubble visible on his shiny scalp. He had the small mean eyes of a snake but the generous mouth of an evangelist. We met those snake oil preachers in Alabama all the time, the ones who promised to deliver you into eternal life if only you'd put *just enough* into their "beggar boxes"—that's what Dad called them, but he'd take a bum before a preacher any day. At least the bums were honest.

The man's shoes squeaked to a stop when he saw us. His eyes widened. But he wasn't looking at me. I followed his gaze.

My father did not appear to notice the man watching him. He dropped the blanket to my shoulders, a stopgap to protect me from the brittle air while we waited for Cherie to live up to her promise of a dry outfit.

"Preston, these nice people got stuck out there on the mountain." Her accent was subtle, a soft twang that eased each word into southern charm. I was so focused on it, I didn't register that she was tugging my shoe off until it caught on my heel and sent white-hot needles shooting through my ankle bone. She winced along with me. "I'm going to wrap her ankle as best I can, but if you could drive them into town—"

"No can do." He shrugged as if this was inconsequential, as if he didn't have an injured child lying on his couch. "Have you looked outside?" The words were aggressive—an accusation, like she was the stupidest person in the world. Then: "Are you wearing makeup?"

Cherie stiffened—of course she did. "Preston, this girl needs a hospital," she said. "We can't let a little rain keep us from helpin' in an emergency."

It was more than a little rain. The storm had gotten worse in the ten minutes since we'd come inside—the lawn had vanished, the rain so thick and heavy it obscured anything beyond the glass panes. The pattering on the roof had become a pounding roar like the predator in the clouds had finally descended to devour us all. I might have been trying to distract myself, but I liked the way those thoughts sounded. Poetic.

But I didn't have time to write poetry about the storm. The baseball had grown to a softball-sized swelling that extended down to my toes, little sausages as wide as they were long. My father stood behind the couch with his fingers wrapped over the back like talons. He stared at Preston. The heady silence made my ribs constrict.

Preston crossed his arms, his gray raincoat squawking, and I was immediately reminded of the crows in the logging field—their screaming. "I didn't mean she doesn't need help. I mean we *can't* get out." His gaze shifted from his wife back to my father. It was strange the way he refused to look at me, as if he was purposefully pretending that I wasn't there. "The tree down at the base of the drive got hit by lightning or something. The whole thing is laid out over the driveway, blocking us in. We're in the soup."

Cherie's pretty forehead wrinkled, but my father's hands relaxed.

I stopped breathing. It wasn't in the way Preston's black eyes twinkled just a little as he said it, and it wasn't in the delivery, though that indicated a lineage outside Tennessee —New York, maybe. No, it was "in the soup" that stuck out as a strange phrase. I'd only heard it once before—well, not heard, but seen in writing.

"How far is it to the road from there?" Dad said, his tone low. The road—of course. They could drive us down to the tree, Dad could carry me around the obstacle and up the street, and then we could flag down a good samaritan to take us to the hospital. Not everyone would be inside during a rainstorm. People liked to tempt fate.

But Preston shook his head again. "The tree's tipped over the bridge, and with the rain, the river's too high to cross on foot." He shrugged one shoulder. "Even if we found a way to the opposite shore, we're the only house for twenty miles. And the radio is callin' 'for tornadoes, y'all."

Y'all. The word was carefully chosen, crafted to indicate southern, but too clumsy to be real. He was doing what my father did—faking it.

But if he were faking, why wouldn't his wife react? Or did he fake it all the time? Dad didn't have to fake with me, but his entire life outside our home was built on pretending to be someone he wasn't.

"Oh dear," Cherie said. She turned to me, her face twisted with earnest concern: eyes narrowed, brow furrowed, lips tight. But her features softened when she met my gaze. "You'll just have to stay here until we can get rid of that tree. I'll get you something dry to wear."

I'll believe that when I see it. But even I didn't appreciate my snark. She was trying to help me—like a mother would—and I was being a jerk. Maybe it was best that I didn't have a mom. I'd be a lot for a mother to handle. And I knew from experience that mothers never lived up to the hype anyway.

She patted my hand again and pushed herself to standing. Thunder clapped.

My father remained still at the back of the couch. "This is my daughter, Poppy," he said, and his tone made my muscles go rigid.

Preston blinked at my dad, steadfastly refusing to acknowledge me.

"I told her not to climb that waterfall, but you know kids." He was covering for me, hiding my clumsiness, but my father's words sounded like a challenge—like he wanted this man to defy him.

The silence that followed was heavier than the clouds.

The hairs along my spine prickled. Though I had no idea why, I got the distinct impression that Preston wanted nothing more than to turn us out into the storm.

"Preston?" Cherie stepped closer to him, head cocked. "Are you okay?" She sounded suspicious, a tightness in her tone that hardened the latter edge of her words. Was she angry at him for being rude to us? Southerners were especially weird about rudeness; they hid their contempt behind phrases like "bless your heart" or "aren't you precious" both of which meant "fuck you." She might be angry at him about something else, though—relationships were troublesome. At the barbecues in Riverside, most grownups watched their partners with thinly veiled contempt. They assumed it was invisible to other people, but few things were invisible to my father. Or to me.

Cherie frowned. "You're staring, Preston."

"Sorry," Preston said, though I couldn't tell if he was talking to her or to my father. Nor could I read the emotion on his face—that was a skill I hadn't yet honed. Some kind of gating mechanism, probably happens a lot in people who grew up with psychopaths. The brain is good at registering the most pressing matters first, and a psychopath at your side forces mundane emotions from your awareness. At least that's what I think happened. At this point, it's hard to say.

"You look familiar," Preston told my dad. "Have we met?"

My father grinned. "I don't think so. Not unless you spend a lot of time in Alabama."

"Alabama, eh?" Preston squinted, but it was another ruse—hiding a deeper emotional response, even I knew that. "Cherie's daddy's from there." He sniffed. "What do you do for work? I swear I've seen you around." Preston's smile was so fake, it might as well have been made of wax.

Thunder growled. The lights flickered, then surged back.

"Serial killer," my father said, his eyes twinkling. "And if you'd seen me around, you'd already be dead."

I stopped breathing.

Preston's jaw dropped. "I'm sorry?"

But then Cherie laughed, a bright exuberant sound that echoed against the walls. It always happened so fast, that shift into laughter. Dad thought it was hilarious how you could tell the truth—the entire brutal truth—and no one would believe you. Though he wasn't usually one to say he was a killer. Dad's teeth glittered in the lamplight. He snickered too.

Preston's face finally softened, and with it, the tightness in my chest. "Okay, fine, point taken." He shook his head and directed his gaze back to his wife. "What should we do now, Cher?"

She bit her lip as if considering, then glanced at me. "I don't think it's broken—probably a bad sprain." I must have looked disbelieving, because she went on, "I'm a nurse."

But nurses didn't make this kind of cash. Was he in medicine too—a skinhead brain surgeon or something? Preston finally met my eyes. "How did you say you got hurt?"

"We were hiking, and I fell on the waterfall," I said. The truth, that I tripped in the dark, didn't seem damning, just embarrassing. But waterfall was what my father told them.

Preston's face flashed, his cheekbones sharper in the flickering light. "The only waterfall I know about is nearly twenty-five miles back on a main hiking trail."

Oops. Dad never should have missed that detail. My injury must have thrown him off.

Preston strode nearer, his feet making wet squelching noises on the hardwood. "Have you ever been to Tennessee before?"

The tension in my back grew more intense. "No." I didn't like the questions. I didn't like that he seemed to be... fishing. I also didn't like the way Preston was staring at my dad again—watching him though he was talking to me. A man who refused to look at a little girl was in many ways more suspicious than one who showed a reasonable amount of blasé interest. I wasn't entirely sure why this felt true, but my father had taught me to listen to my gut. "My ankle really hurts," I said. "I don't want to talk anymore."

"But—"

"You heard her." My father moved around the couch, putting himself between me and Preston, a wall of muscled defense. My spine relaxed, the tendons loosening, and the straining pressure through my shoulders eased. "If her ankle doesn't need an emergency room, and the ladies have the dry clothes under control, I think there's only one thing left to do: Let's light up the grill." He chuckled—kidding, I was almost sure.

"Grab the chainsaw while you're out there, Preston," Cherie said, returning to the couch. "And if you can't get the tree moved today, I'll set Poppy up in Jeremy's room, and her father in the spare."

Preston's face fell. "She can take our room," he snapped.

Jeremy? Was someone else living here? And what was wrong with Jeremy's room?

Cherie frowned at her husband. "Preston—"

"Fine, okay? Of course that makes sense." He smiled again—but too intensely, too *happy*, fake-happy—and dropped his gaze to me once more. A glance only, but in that split second, the interest in his eyes made my skin crawl.

Ah. It wasn't that something was wrong with Jeremy's room.

Something was really, *really* wrong with Preston.

CHAPTER NINE

My father left me with Cherie and headed out through the back archway; hopefully he'd have the tree hacked apart in a few hours. Cherie gave me a Tylenol, then carefully sliced my tattered athletic pants to the knee and cleaned my leg with a bowl of warm soapy water. Preston had gone with Dad, and I felt his absence like a thorn pulled from a wound —relief. He was sick, somehow, I was sure, even if I didn't know what darkness he was hiding.

Unless it was all in my head, another clue to a puzzle that didn't exist. It was hard to tell sometimes.

"Brave, brave girl. I can't believe you fell climbing up a waterfall," she murmured softly as she applied antibacterial cream to a few abrasions I hadn't noticed along the outer edge of my heel.

She shouldn't believe it—it was a lie. But it wasn't worth arguing the point; she had no concept of what bravery was. Plus, I didn't *want* to argue with her. About anything. Cherie's fingers were warm and soft, her movements delicate. I did not tense at the scissors in her hand. She wrapped my ankle in a gauzy fabric bandage with quick deft movements, tightly enough to make my toes a little numb. But the pressure... it helped. When she offered me her hand, I pulled myself up, though she shook her head when I leaned against my bad leg. "Easy, baby."

Baby. I was *not* a baby, but it struck me how much it felt like she was treating me as her child.

I leaned against Cherie's shoulder, listening to the hammering rain as we stumbled through the living room. Was this what it was like to have a mother? A real, fully capable mother? But that was a pipe dream; I didn't think a mother existed who'd understand us—who could understand Dad. Sharon had tried, and it hadn't ended well. It was better for us to be alone. Better for everyone.

At the back of the house, beyond the piano, was a long hallway wide enough for a thin table, an oil painting above it of cherub children playing in a stream. Cherie pointed at the door across from the table—"We'll put your Dad right in there"—then showed me to the first door, her arm looped under my armpits. "Are you scared, honey?"

I shook my head. If I was scared, it meant I didn't trust my father, and what kind of daughter would that make me?

The hinge creaked—loud. I frowned at it, then surveyed the infamous "Jeremy's room," which turned out to be larger than our living room at home, with space for a wraparound desk, a chest of drawers, and a king-sized bed too large for even the biggest of children. But it was definitely a child's room, though I'd seen no other evidence of a child, no family photos in the living room, no stray toys. A nightlight sat on the oak dresser: an opaque *Star Wars* ship the size of my head.

The carpet was soft and blue like the ocean. Cherie eased me down onto the bed, *Teenage Mutant Ninja Turtles* sheets that felt strangely dusty. *Huh.* Was the boy at camp? A stepchild, perhaps, currently staying with the other parent?

Cherie headed for the closet; the mirrored door slid open with a *shh* that might have been my brain telling me to stop overthinking. She returned with new sheets and a fluffy blanket the color of sand, the fleece better suited for deep winter than the muggy vestiges of summer. Ocean floors and sandy blankets. And weapon-wielding cartoon turtles.

"Do you like *Star Wars*?" she asked. It seemed she'd caught me looking at the nightlight. "My son's favorite—Preston's too."

I had never seen *Star Wars*. I nodded. No wonder she seemed like a good mom—she was a mom, probably had a lot of practice. But there was something off about the room. That hinge... why wouldn't they fix the hinge? Why wouldn't they wash the grimy sheets? It felt like a piece to a larger puzzle—a hint in a treasure hunt.

But sometimes a hinge was just a hinge. Sometimes a ribbon was just a ribbon.

She nodded to my propped leg. "If you don't want to wrestle sweatpants over that, I have some sundresses that might fit you. If they're too big, I'm sure I can find a sweater for you to wear over top. Whatever makes you comfortable."

Comfortable—that was always the thing that my father said clothes should be. That I should never dress for anyone else. But Preston's creepy eyes flashed in my brain, and I stifled a shudder. Hiding inside a sweater did seem like a good idea.

"Sorry if it's dusty," she said, glancing at the furniture. "I'll run a rag over the dressers, and we can light a candle if you need one. I'd air it out, but—" She gestured to the window that looked out over the back of the house, all rain-soaked woods and blue-gray mountains.

"It's perfect," I said slowly, raising my voice above the storm. "And if your son comes home, I can sleep on the couch." I watched her face carefully; I had a hunch about the squealing hinge. Was it a clue? Or was I wrong again?

"Jeremy..." She swallowed hard. "Jeremy won't be coming home. He died last winter." The grief in her voice was palpable.

Lightning zinged across the sky, brightening the room in stark white for a split second before the lights flickered off.

This time, the room stayed dark.

"I'll go get you those sundresses," Cherie said. "Hopefully the power comes back on soon. Maybe we can pull out the Monopoly board." But her voice was strained.

She didn't believe the lights would come back on any more than I did.

CHAPTER TEN

I STARED AT THE CEILING, watching the lightning flicker in shuddering bursts against Jeremy's pale walls. Day or night, it all felt the same. The cinnamon candle Cherie had put in the room to combat the dust tickled my nose with its sweet-spicy reek. I wanted to nap, to pass the time until they cleared the tree or until the storm was over, but I couldn't.

It wasn't the pain in my ankle, though that certainly didn't help. Two hours after we'd arrived, and my leg was already improving, truth be told. A bad sprain, probably. Like Cherie said. My stomach hurt, too, an oily squeezing sensation that spurred intermittent nausea. Stupid Lunch-ables. Darn Squeeze-Its.

But the unease was mostly in my head, a quiet but incessant nagging that kept me in limbo between rest and wakefulness, and not in the relaxed way of the truck's window—itchy inside my brain. I was so *itchy*.

I sighed and shifted, wincing when I caught my leg on the blanket. The storm continued its assault on the windows; the thunder growled enough to rattle the doors in the frames. I think that was why I didn't hear him right away.

"Poppy?" Just a whisper of breath. From outside the room.

Dad? I sat up, but I couldn't tell if there was a shadow beneath the door with the way the candle tossed its jaundiced glow against the baseboards. The silence stretched. Had I imagined the sound? But then the whisper came again: "Poppy?"

The doorknob rattled.

That was when I knew it wasn't my father. He had never once burst into my room without permission. He always said it was my decision what happened to my body, and that extended to the spaces I claimed, no matter how temporarily. I was glad I'd turned the bolt.

I eased myself off the mattress, prepared for that familiar throbbing in my leg, but I felt only a dull ache in my ankle, like the pull of a sore muscle as I limped toward the door.

"Who's there?" I knew the answer, but I was buying time. The room spun more than it should have. I leaned my head against the doorjamb, listening hard, trying to get my bearings. The storm spit against the glass, and for a moment the room fluttered with a brilliant pulsing white.

"It's Preston—Mr. Shaw."

Shaw. Was that their last name? I should have felt threatened, and another child might have, but I wasn't just any child. I was Poppy Pratt, my father's daughter, almost grown and smart enough to tackle anything—and anyone. I was better than a stupid roach even if it had startled me. Better than a pile of rocks even if they'd tripped me up. Better than a ribbon though I'd been wrong about its meaning.

I stood straighter, heaving my body off the door. The dizziness tugged at me, especially after I popped the lock, but I gritted my teeth against it.

The hinge shrieked when I eased the door open, as if begging me to slam it closed once more. But it was always better to know what you were up against. He clearly came here for a reason.

Preston's silhouette blended into the background, shadow on shadow in the darkened hallway, mere feet from the doorjamb. I tried to plaster on a smile, and his shoulders relaxed a little. I was only nine, after all. Unassuming. Innocent.

"I know you didn't fall down a waterfall, Poppy." His voice was a hiss—pressured—but loud enough to be heard even if he stepped away. Why was he standing so close? To make sure I didn't slam the door in his face? "Your camping equipment is barely three miles from here. I looked."

He went to our campsite? How'd he sneak off without my father noticing? But that was ridiculous. My father would have noticed—he saw everything.

"What does your dad do for a living?" Preston asked.

That's what you're here to ask me? Because you want me to say something besides serial killer? "He does a lot of charity work," I said. Everyone loved a guy who gave back.

"That's not a job. But he runs funeral homes, right?" Preston sniffed. "He have lots of spare time, running funeral homes? Time to travel?"

I glanced up the hall, at the door to the room where they'd put my father—no movement. He wasn't in it, or he would have come out by now. I leveled my gaze at Preston and waited in the dark. I wasn't one to walk into a trap by confirming or denying—Dad had taught me better than that. And the funeral home thing... I wasn't sure what my father's angle was. It made sense for Dad to invent an occupation since "do-gooder" was, as Preston correctly stated, not a job. But telling someone you were a funeral home director or a mortician... those were jobs that made you look like a weirdo. Those made people upset. Dad wouldn't choose that without a reason. "You can talk to my father about his work, but I'd think anyone who runs a funeral home would have time to spare. Dead people don't waste time with talking."

He frowned. "Have you ever seen my wife around your house in Alabama?"

I raised an eyebrow. Why would I have seen Cherie? We didn't even live in the same state. "I think you should ask my father any questions you have. Or your wife."

The silence was a cloud thicker and darker than those raging beyond the windows. I could hear his unspoken protest in my head, knew without a doubt that he'd already asked my father, had asked his wife. He was here because he thought I was a dumb kid. But he didn't know me. And he certainly didn't know my father, or he wouldn't have let us in.

"Preston?" Another voice, from the hall at his back. Cherie emerged from the shadows, wafting into being as if formed of mist and candlelight from the cinnamon votive at my back. "Poppy needs her rest." Cherie's voice was cold and laced with finality.

Preston stiffened. "She shouldn't be in there," he said.

"It's only for one night, Preston—"

"Fine, fine." He raised his hands in a "whoa" gesture and backed away from my door. "No need to borrow trouble." He pushed past Cherie and strode down the hall.

Borrow trouble? What a stupid idiom. My pen pal liked it too. But the idea that one could borrow trouble meant you could give it back, and I was pretty sure trouble didn't work that way.

Cherie followed, mumbling something at him, but I couldn't tell what she was saying. They vanished into the darkened hallway. Their bedroom door slammed, and the moment the lock clicked, her voice rose, a sharp high bark followed by Preston's pressured tenor: "She shouldn't be in there, that's Jeremy's—"

That was the last line I understood, the words devolving into a frantic give and take, but there was no mistaking the anger in their voices. But their arguing wasn't the problem—that wasn't what kept me rooted to the spot, standing against the jamb, staring at their bedroom door.

Why would a grown man be knocking on my door, trying to ambush me? What was he trying to find out about us?

And where the hell was my father?

CHAPTER ELEVEN

A CRASH from the back bedroom jolted me out of my stupor. How long had I stood leaning against the doorjamb? I slunk back into the bedroom and locked the door quietly behind me, but I could still hear Preston and Cherie—louder now. Yelling, though the door obscured the words. It wasn't the words that were bothering me anyway. The hairs between my shoulders were prickling, an intense sensation like needles on my back.

My father was not quick to anger—I'd never seen him so much as raise his voice, and the display of being bodily out of control unnerved me. It wasn't safe to trust someone who might lose control, and Preston was clearly capable if the yelling and that crashing bang were any indication.

I doubted Preston was upset that I was sleeping in his dead son's room. Anyone would understand grief—had Preston explained about Jeremy, my father would have nodded solemnly and suggested that we sleep on the couches, or just shared the spare room where he was sleeping. We didn't need that much privacy while we waited for the storm to pass.

But Preston's eyes hadn't gone glassy with sadness. He'd agreed with Cherie that I should take the room. He'd even smiled—*pretended*. Because he wanted to make sure it didn't look suspicious. So why would avoiding suspicion be more critical than any emotions aroused by the memory of his dead child?

There could be something in this room worth hiding: some clue, something incriminating. Something secret. What was it that Preston didn't want me to find? From the sound of their raised voices, it seemed like he'd actually started to panic.

The fabric of Cherie's T-shirt felt itchy against my skin; even the oversized sweatpants I'd hauled on were chilly. But for the first time since we'd gotten here, I had something more pressing than the pain in my ankle to focus on: I had a mission. I was tired of being wrong, and if I was wrong about this, no one ever had to know. But if I was right...

I started with the desk. Easy, maybe too obvious for a man like Preston, but he seemed cocky—perhaps cocky enough to assume no one would bother to search in the first place. The overly confident often hid things in plain sight.

It was easier to hobble with the bandage wrapped so tightly, but my foot ached again in pulsing beats that matched the throb of blood in my head. The sounds from Cherie's bedroom had faded into the background. I leaned heavily on the wall and then the desk, a bulky antique with even grooves cut into the wood from the desktop to the clawfoot legs. There were crayons in the top right drawer, and markers in the left along with a coloring book and a tiny flashlight no wider than my thumb—that might come in handy later, but I didn't want them to see the light beneath the door now. Didn't want them to know I was investigating. The front of the drawer and the top edge of the desk were heavily nicked, tiny pockmarks of damage. I ran my hand over the divots and peered at my fingertips; even in the gloom I could see the shiny graphite residue. Pencil. Jeremy stabbed his pretty desk, that unappreciative little punk.

But pencil nicks and coloring books were not what Preston was hiding. I turned my back on the desk and scanned the room. During the last treasure hunt my father created, I'd found the fairy house well back in the woods, only a few broken stalks of wildflowers to lead me there. The injured flowers might have been from a passing deer, but the broken stalks were too uniform, too small. Deliberate. He'd hidden the house in the hollow of an oak marked by a single snapped branch way up high—too thick to break beneath the weight of a raccoon or a squirrel, but not too thick to crack under the boot of a clumsy human. Now I realize that those hints were the main lessons—a broken twig or a snapped flower stalk were good ways to figure out if someone was watching you. If the sheriff had been poking around, I might register a single mangled sunflower, or the uneven edge of a booted footprint, or the tiniest scratch in a tree's bark that might indicate someone leaning against it.

The little things were the giveaways.

But in Cherie's house, I wasn't sure what normal looked like. Were the slightly askew hangers in the closet the mark of someone hiding forbidden items behind them? It did not appear so—nothing on the closet floor save a stack of puzzle boxes and assorted board games. Two sets of Candyland. That seemed strange, having two of the same game, but there was nothing untoward hiding beneath either cardboard lid, just plastic game tokens, their respective cardboard landscapes folded on top, one shiny, one worn—well-used. Nothing weird in the puzzles; nothing unusual in the

Monopoly box either unless you found the celebration of capitalism strange. Which I did. Even then, I knew that humans had an almost ravenous desire to destroy each other, and it was always easier to do if you owned a whole mess of hotels.

I stacked the boxes neatly and clawed my way to standing on the closet's doorjamb. What else? What was out of place?

Was the flattened carpet beneath the dresser from someone slamming the drawer too hard while trying to hide incriminating evidence, or had they moved the furniture to redecorate? I limped my way along, grinding my teeth when I leaned too hard against my injured foot, but there was nothing beneath the dresser. Of course there wasn't. That would have been too easy, like the desk.

The top drawer of the bureau did not squeal, not the way the bedroom door did. Inside, little boy underwear was stacked in even rows, socks that wouldn't cover half of my foot. But no duct tape or handcuffs. Nothing suspicious.

The voices in the next room rose again. Preston's wife certainly seemed to think that he was unstable—why else would she be so immediately suspicious of her husband knocking on a visitor's door? He could have been asking if I needed a snack or another blanket. Did she... think he was a pedophile?

Yeah, I know... it was all a stretch, broad strokes of conjecture. Blame the creativity of children. But these ideas seeming unlikely didn't mean I was wrong.

I slid the top drawer shut and moved on to the next: T-shirts. Shorts. Little boy cartoon characters, more *Teenage Mutant Ninja Turtles*. A child frozen in time. How old was little Jeremy when he died? From the state of the room, normal clothes and toys, no indication of medical accommodations, it had not been a prolonged natural death from cancer or disease—something sudden.

I slammed the bottom drawer harder than the others and winced. *Oops.* Maybe I was wasting my time. Maybe Preston was just a jerk, and there was nothing to find. But... no, this wasn't right. I was missing something; I felt it from the roots of my teeth all the way down to the pulsing in my swollen toes. *Can't be too careful, right, Dad?*

There were no end tables, nothing beside the bed. Wouldn't want little Jeremy to roll the wrong way and smash his head on the corner of the table and die. Was that what had happened to him? Something boring and not at all suspicious? Maybe he'd choked on an action figure.

I clutched the headboard—carved finials that matched the even grooves on the dresser and the desk—and slid gingerly down the wall, my foot out to the side to avoid knocking it. But even using the muscles in my upper leg made my ankle throb.

I ignored the ache. I stretched out on my belly and peered beneath the bed. Little boy shoes sat near the footboard. I fingered the tied laces—seemed Jeremy had slipped them off for the last time, and his mother didn't have the heart to unravel the last thing he ever did with his pudgy fingers.

I replaced the shoes beneath the dust ruffle and pushed myself up onto my palms, my nose nearly touching the mattress. The sticky comforter was gone, replaced by the sand-colored fleece blanket that barely lapped over the edge, exposing the lower lip of the mattress pad. That's the reason I noticed it—a tiny spot near the lower seam where the fitted sheet was folded over oddly. A touch bowed, a little wrinkled, that was all. Almost imperceptible. Like a broken flower stem.

My heart hammered, my ankle forgotten as I slipped my hand beneath the mattress. I dug around, back and forth, wiggling my fingertips, but felt only cloth. Was I wrong?

No... *there*.

Electricity sang through my veins. My fingers brushed the edge of something cold and dry—paper. I slid it from beneath the sheets with a hissing sound like an angry snake. Several pieces of construction paper atop a large manila envelope.

I squinted at the top page, a drawing scrawled in crude shaky lines—mom, dad, and child. *Huh*. I'm not sure what I expected, but this wasn't it. A stick figure of a boy with a cartoon frown and a bright blue tear on his cheek stood on the right side of the page, limbs and fingers done in black wax, jagged lines pressed so hard into the paper they'd torn through at the ends. Pointed triangles for eyebrows. The stick boy had spiky yellow hair the same color as the curls on the stick-figure woman at his side, her face also haggard with sadness, a stark contrast to the bald man in the middle of the picture—he wore a smile. Stranger still, both mom and child stood in a lake of blood, unless it was some weird crimson grass. There was certainly no source of the blood—no victim.

I set the first drawing aside. The second page was in the same vein: a small dog, like a Chihuahua, lying on the ground, Xs over his eyes. More of that red earth. The dog might be construed as the victim if he'd had any wounds on him, but again, there were no overt indications of violence. Just the dead dog, and the sad faces of the boy and the woman. But... I blinked at the page in my hand again, then at the one on the bed. In both drawings, the stick-figure man was smiling. And that wasn't the only difference. The woman and the boy were drawn in black, just a series of jagged limbs, but Preston—I assumed it was Preston—was wearing clothes, blue jeans and orange T-shirts.

Yeah, that felt like a clue to something. The child had clearly been traumatized, his mother too. And if Preston had been abusing Jeremy, Cherie might not have known the extent even if her gut told her not to let him knock on bedroom doors. There was a girl at my school whose father was molesting her—her mom had no idea. But my dad knew because of how Abilene walked... whatever that meant. A month later, Abilene's father had left town, and Dad bought her mom groceries for a few months until she got a secretary job at the sheriff's station.

I had no idea where Abilene's dad had moved, but it was good that she smiled more now.

I set the pages on top of the bed. Those drawings, as illuminating as they might have been, were less interesting than the envelope beneath them. It was too heavy for just illustrations or even coloring books, and when I ran a finger down the back side, I could feel the spaces—thick and uniform. Whatever was inside was broken at regular inter-vals, like stacks of index cards. Perhaps photos of the child, though they seemed too small for that. Cherie and Preston didn't have a single remembrance of the boy anywhere but this room, a virtual shrine to the kid, everything exactly as he'd left it.

The top flap of the envelope was secured with a string. I unwound it carefully. This might be nothing more than an extension of the shrine—baseball cards, or his favorite comics.

From down the hall, Cherie's voice roared, then Preston's booming response. The shouting accelerated, a loud, long burst of frantic noises, some that sounded more like screams, then a horrific crashing sound like one of them had thrown a vase. And then... silence.

I unwound faster. The string came free.

Whoa. Not index cards, not baseball cards. Money. A lot of it, all bundled up in paper bands. My lungs opened, the air suddenly more breathable. *I knew it.*

I didn't need to ask why Preston would hide it here. Normal people assigned meaning to the items belonging to a lost loved one—they wouldn't disturb that sanctuary by rifling through it. People who felt things didn't use a dead child's bedroom as a cover.

It was the kind of thing my father would do.

No, I hadn't proven that Preston was a bad guy. So far. But he had a hidden stash of bills—he had an escape plan, and only someone who had done something illegal needed an escape plan. Besides, the money, those drawings hidden away... If he had done something to the boy, that explained his reluctance to have me in Jeremy's room. Cherie's nervousness when he spoke to me. And it had to be Preston's cash; Cherie wouldn't have put me in this room if she knew about the money, wouldn't have laid me right on top of it. Plus, he'd come to Jeremy's room with a series of strange questions—an excuse to see if I'd found his stash?

Once the sun came out, and the phones were back working, and the lights came on, we'd leave. I'd never see Preston and Cherie again.

I had until the storm passed to uncover all of Preston's dirty secrets. I had a day, maybe a little more to search the house. I didn't know how many steps it might take to find the treasure I sought, but I was good at the hunt. I was very good.

I paused only briefly to glance at the drawings—the man smiling while Jeremy and his mother cried. Then I secured the top of the envelope once more and slipped that and the pictures back into their hiding place.

But for two slowly pulsing heartbeats, I could not bring myself to recover the exposed edge of the mattress. The child was dead, and that thought stuck in my brain like a barb from a Sweetgum tree. Preston had clearly abused Jeremy. But had the man killed his child? That lake of blood, the Xs over the dog's eyes, the already grieving mother...

It made sense if Jeremy saw it coming. Children often did.

CHAPTER TWELVE

Despite my newfound determination to discover what Preston was hiding, the moment I sat back down on the bed, my eyelids drooped like I'd swallowed a bottle of Benadryl. But it was a fitful kind of rest. Just the thought of the money hidden beneath my prone form made me like the girl in *The Princess and the Pea*. I imagined I could feel the envelope there, the mattress lumpy beneath my shoulder. I imagined I could smell the cash above the cinnamon smoke.

Cherie's soft knock pulled me from half-sleep, but unlike Preston, she did not try the knob before I roused myself and unlocked the door. Her mouth was turned down at the corners, her eyes hollow in a way that reminded me of the drawing—desperation, the eyes of someone irrevocably stuck. Young Jeremy was quite astute. But was Cherie? Did she know about the pictures?

Unfortunately, those questions would have to wait. Fresh scratches marred the back of her right hand. She'd applied makeup to cover what must have been redness on her face, the swelling along her jaw. She'd redone her mascara, too, and straightened her blue eyeliner. That was the era, that blue eyeliner, though rich women went navy instead of cerulean like the redneck girls hanging out the back of their daddy's pickup.

She sat beside me on the bed and lifted the hem of the sweatpants to check the swelling at my shin. She didn't so much as glance at the bed. If she knew about the money, she would have looked. Maybe Preston was adept enough to conceal all evidence of Jeremy's pictures too—why else would they be hidden in a mattress? Why keep them at all? Just to reminisce about the way he'd hurt his family?

"He hit you?" I asked, though it wasn't a question.

Cherie swallowed hard. "Don't you worry about me, dear. Leave all that for the grown-ups."

My hackles rose. I wasn't all the way grown, but I was perfectly capable of knowing that what he did to her was wrong. "People who love you don't hit you."

She said nothing to this, but her hands were shaking as she tugged the pants back down over my ankle, pressed another Tylenol into my hand, and then helped me out into the hall with the promise of food. But I hesitated as we neared the living room. "Is Preston—"

"He won't be joining us." Her tone was frosty, as bitter as lemon rind, but her words sent the warm vibration of relief seeping through my blood. I didn't want to see Preston again until I knew exactly what he was. I'd discovered his go-bag within minutes of searching that bedroom. What might I find elsewhere in this house?

It was an entirely new kind of treasure hunt, one more pertinent and vital than any I'd experienced. My veins vibrated like well-struck guitar strings as I limped through the living area. Could I prove he'd killed the boy? I didn't think Cherie would tell me the truth—she wouldn't even admit he'd hit her. And working with only half the truth—

without proof—felt like cheating. If Preston was guilty, I needed to know exactly how guilty before I decided what to tell my father. I figured he'd blackmail Preston with the information I uncovered. Rich as Preston was, we'd be set for years.

And the best part was, we could save Cherie from her maniac of a husband.

I could save her. But I couldn't afford to be wrong. Not again.

Cherie settled me at the enormous kitchen island, my feet dangling off the bar stool. My father was there, too, wearing sweatpants like mine and a T-shirt just a touch too tight. It was his shoulders; he was sturdier than Preston. Stronger. Where the heck had he been when they were throwing punches in the bedroom? He had to have been outside still—he'd never sit by and listen to a woman get beaten, I was positive on that. Yes, he was out in the storm. Alone in the... wildly raging storm. Working on the tree, surely.

My father smiled at me from in front of the giant stone oven that stood tall and proud along the back wall—I had been right about what it was from the outside. Yeah, I was good. But I'd been wrong about the archway from the living area only leading to the kitchen and the pool house. This space beyond the arch was another world, one as lavish as the living room.

I could see a dining room through another open arch at the back, fit for a dozen suit-clad guests—a long wooden table topped with empty ceramic vases that probably held lilies during parties. The pool house lay to the right, accessible through a wide hallway that also contained Preston's office; I could see the checkerboard glass of his office doors from the kitchen island. No sign of Preston himself, though. No noises from down the hall. Nothing but the rain.

"This house is really nice," I said. I was trying to feel her out, glean all the information I could before I made any decisions. I wanted to help her, I think—or maybe I wanted a mother, and in some strange way it felt like I had one to protect during those days in the mountains. Those mommy issues would be my therapist's guess. But shrinks always like to focus on your parents; they miss that sometimes, you're a selfish asshole. Memory is funny like that, and my guesses about what I might have thought at nine are probably wrong.

Cherie smiled and patted my hand. "Thank you so much, dear. I do my best, but there's always something going wrong in a place this size."

The rain outside was a whooshing scream that harangued the wide kitchen window and tore at the ferns on either side of the pool's wrought iron gate.

Cherie glanced that way and sighed. "There will be a lot of work to do when this is over. The toilet in the pool house is broken too."

"I can take a look at that," my father said.

She shook her head firmly. "It's already been a month. I'll get a plumber out."

A month? People with this kind of money didn't wait to fix simple plumbing problems. People with money picked up the phone and made the problem go away. Maybe Preston didn't want a plumber wandering around his house; strangers could be dangerous if you had secrets. My father always fixed things himself, too, but he enjoyed working with his hands.

"Come on, Cherie," he said. "It'll help me earn our keep since I can't move that tree alone."

Preston had stopped helping then? Maybe he knew my father would give him shit for hurting Cherie. But my dad should still be out there working. He should still be trying, right? And yet... I hadn't heard a chainsaw all day. No thud of an ax. And he was cooking inside and not on the grill the way he'd joked about when we first arrived. Where in the world had he been?

"I'm... sorry about Preston," Cherie said. "I'm sure he'll be willing to help soon."

My father shrugged. "It's okay. Not your fault." He gestured to the closed oven where I could hear the meat popping clear through the stone; I could imagine the grease, leaking like sweat from its pores. "More for us, right?"

It was strange how domestic it felt. Just a mom and a dad and a kid preparing dinner in a thunderstorm.

"What does Preston do for a living?" I cut in. Despite Cherie's vocation, I no longer thought he was a medical professional; if he was, he'd know how to hurt her without leaving bruises. Maybe a high-powered attorney. Those guys knew how to keep a battered woman under their thumb, just like cops—sheriffs, deputies, anyone in law enforcement. I was young, but it was easy enough to tell which kids were getting beaten at home, which mothers were scared of their husbands. But cops didn't make this kind of money unless they were crooked; cocaine paid better than handcuffing motorists for DUIs.

Cherie looked away, at Preston's office, and my father raised an eyebrow at me—*What are you up to, Poppy?* But he settled it down into place before she turned back.

"He's an investor," Cherie said. "Mostly technology stuff. People say that computers are the way of the future, but I don't see it." She shrugged. "Hasn't stopped them from paying him though."

My father chuckled and pulled open the cast iron door of the oven. Without air conditioning to temper it, the heat pricked at my forehead and raised beads of sweat along my hairline.

"Computers always seemed silly to me," my father said to the interior of the stove. "I like the personal touch: talking face to face, none of those darn emails or whatever they're called." I could smell the flames—the smoke. The salt of sizzling flesh.

Cherie nodded. "Agreed. I'd be perfectly happy here without any technology at all."

She liked her life... simple? That was good. Maybe she wouldn't be hard to save from her abusive husband, not if she could walk away from this place—from all the money. I could tell her about the cash, too; Dad and I didn't need it, and he'd find a way to get whatever we did need out of Preston. She could take the hidden money and run.

And as my father turned the meat over the coals, another thought took root deep in my mind: Maybe she could even... come home with us.

No—crazy, that's crazy. But that didn't stop me from considering it.

Cherie set the island with porcelain dishes and shining flatware that was probably real silver, then sat at one side of the island with her plate of grilled pork, my father across from her on his stool. We ate an early dinner by candlelight, the flames flickering off the walls and making their faces shimmer with an almost ghostly radiance. They heated croissants from the freezer, and tonged fresh greens into a carved wooden bowl. She even put our water in tall crystal glasses, too ornate for a blackout-storm meal. The ambiance was better suited to a romantic evening.

I picked at my salad and ate croissants, pillowy layers of

butter and sweet chewy dough. Why didn't Cherie seem upset? Wasn't that strange for a woman who was just punched in the face by her husband? Maybe not if she was used to it. But I couldn't be sure—my father didn't hit women.

"Are you okay?" Cherie asked. I nodded, but she wasn't looking at me.

My dad was staring back at her, his eyes hooded. "Fine, fine. It's just... you remind me of Poppy's mother," he said.

I lowered my croissant. He almost never mentioned my mother; she was a drug addict, left right after I was born. It was strange to even hear the word on his lips.

Cherie did not see it as strange—she raised an eyebrow and winked. "I assume that's a compliment?"

My father nodded. "Of course it is. She was a wonderful woman too." So charming. Her cheeks flushed pink.

Is he hitting on her? That didn't make sense, unless he wanted a friendly connection to a wealthy woman. He always had an angle.

I watched his face, trying to decipher what his motives might be. He seemed a little sleepy, the way his eyelids were drooping. But then he straightened; his eyes were back to normal when he gestured to the archway, to the living area. "Which one of you plays piano?" he asked Cherie. "That's a very pretty instrument."

"I've played since I was a little girl." She took a bite of pork, but then her eyes widened—excitement? My father wasn't often excited, so that was a tricky emotion for me to discern in other people. But I knew I was right when her head snapped my way. "Let me teach you, Poppy!" She grinned with all her teeth, but in the yellowed glare of the candlelight, it looked like a grimace. "We'll have some time while these boys are clearing that tree out of the way, and I haven't had a new student in a decade."

"You taught piano too?" My father cut his eyes at me. "What a lucky break for us."

"Yeah... lucky," I echoed, but it felt strange for him to be asking questions. In Riverside, my father knew everything about everyone. He was the one who held on to the secrets —who always knew what strings to pull. Here, we were out of our element. Here, we were the outsiders. Or he was.

Here... I knew more than he did. I knew about the money, about the weird drawings. I was the one with the secrets.

Me and Preston.

CHAPTER THIRTEEN

It was too dark to investigate the house once the sun went down—a flashlight would garner unwanted attention, and in the hushed silence of night, I'd be all the more conspicuous stumbling around the living area.

There was nothing else of interest in Jeremy's room, so I locked myself in and dozed off and on, listening for the scraping of shoes on the floor outside the bedroom or the squeal of the doorknob, the moaning creak of the unoiled hinge—Preston surely had a key. Nothing. No snoring from the back bedroom either, nor sounds of Preston digging through the fridge after the rest of us had left the room. There was only the rain and the wind whipping against the roof.

My brain felt sludgy, the hours passing too slowly, like wading through pudding. Where was Preston? The cash remained in the envelope beneath the mattress—I'd checked before I climbed onto the bed—so he hadn't run off yet. He was probably sleeping in the pool house or in his office. I hoped he had to sleep on the floor, cold and uncomfortable.

I wished my ankle felt better so I could sneak in and put a spider in his mouth.

With that thought in my head, I finally fell asleep.

I think the clattering of dishes is what woke me. It was barely dawn, but Cherie was doing something in the kitchen, humming while she worked, probably cleaning up after our meal. Very... homemaker-y. Maternal.

I slid from the bed, testing my leg against the floor, and rubbed at my chest—too tight. My ribs felt like a cage; the room was a prison. I strained my ears, wondering if Preston was playing guard outside the room, but there were no sounds of breath, no shadows seeping beneath the door. Good. I had no time to waste.

Little things. Broken stems. My skin itched with the desire to seek out clues.

I grabbed the flashlight from Jeremy's desk drawer and stuck it in the pocket of my sweatpants. I pulled my shoes on, too, wincing—a little damp, but with the laces tied up tight, they helped to stabilize my bad ankle. I only had an hour, maybe two, to poke around before they started looking for me. So where would Preston hide his secrets?

I thought I knew where to start.

The hinge squealed, and I froze, my hand locked on the knob. But no one came to investigate the sound. I didn't hear the clattering in the kitchen anymore, so I limp-slid my way from the bedroom up the hall, through the main living area, listening, listening, and peered around the corner. Cherie was not in the kitchen—probably straightening another room, perhaps sweeping up the glass in her bedroom after last night's brawl. *Lucky break.* I lurched as fast as I was able past the kitchen island, then into the hallway on the other side.

Preston's office was marked by double doors covered in

windows that offered a hash-marked view of the desk inside. Not a lot of privacy, but the seemingly open nature could lull his wife into a false sense of security. I listened for another breath to the house—just the rain beating the windows—and closed the door softly behind me.

The desk here was carved wood, though the legs weren't smooth like those of the marble table in the living room. Elephants, gray and stately, their trunks licking at the floor, balanced a giant oval of glass on their triangular ears and wide heads. A boxy looking computer covered most of the desktop. Four small drawers; I'd deal with those in a moment.

Along the back wall was a giraffe sofa table topped with a vase, the painting of a pond tacked to the wall above it. I ran my hand beneath the tabletop in case he'd taped something to the bottom, but nada. No filing cabinets in here either, which cut down the number of places I had to search. His chair smelled of cologne, a strange acidic musk that tingled in my nostrils when I eased down into it.

I booted up the computer first. A screen popped up, demanding a password—crap. I should have asked when they got married, when Jeremy's birthday was, or Preston's mother's maiden name—very inconspicuous. I tried "Jeremy" and "Cherie" and "PrestonShaw" and "IAm-AMegaAsshole," but all were wrong. I turned it off. I was already screwing up. But while I was here...

The shape of the desk made the upper drawers more artistic than functional. The upper right-hand drawer held only highlighters, a Zippo, and a pack of Kools; on the other side were two more packs of cigarettes and a crayon drawing of a turtle, bright green under a yellow sun. No jagged lines or stick figures. Of course the joyful image was the one he'd kept accessible. Preston couldn't very well show his colleagues pictures of stick men and dead dogs and lakes of blood.

The lower drawers slid open with a *cshhhh*. Not locked. A dead end, surely; who would hide something questionable in a wide-open drawer? Perhaps I was wasting my—

I stopped short, my hand resting on the files in the lower drawer in a decidedly suspicious way. The water in the kitchen was running again—Cherie was back. That was quick. I doubted she'd gone looking for me and found the room empty; it was far too early to risk knocking, six o'clock at the latest. I strained my ears, and when the clattering in the kitchen began again, my shoulders relaxed. She'd probably gone to take out the trash—that made sense. And if she found me here...

Sorry, Cherie, I got lost, I practiced in my head. *I was looking for a pencil, thought I might draw a picture.*

I rifled through the files in the bottom drawer: bank statements, the receipt for a riding lawnmower, a folder full of business cards. What did I expect? A sticky note with "Reminder: Kill Jeremy" scrawled on it in block letters? I flipped the corner of the rug just in case—it's where I might have hidden something valuable, something secret. I even checked behind the painting, then inside the vase, but there was nothing here to find.

I retreated to the hall, a little ashamed of myself—I was wasting time I didn't have. The running water had stopped again, but the clattering hadn't. Could I get through the kitchen without her seeing me? Maybe. If I got caught, I could tell her I got up early, went exploring like any curious child might. But there was still one other place in this section of the house I hadn't looked.

The glass doors from the office let through a significant amount of light, the hazy gray spilling onto the hallway floor and washing out the dark wood. But the door at the far end of the hallway was steeped in shadow.

The pool house lay beyond. I started that way, but it suddenly occurred to me that perhaps the pool house itself was not the most critical location I had yet to explore. I was still going the right way, though, if there was a door to the outside—a door to the driveway where Preston was refusing to work on that tree. Why would he do that? Just to avoid my Dad? That seemed thin.

A broken tree—a broken stem?

The skin between my shoulder blades prickled. There would be time to investigate the pool house later. But if I wanted to look at that tree, I had to do it before anyone knew I was gone; adults didn't let injured children go wandering around in thunderstorms.

I limped toward the pool house, leaning heavily against the wall. Unlike Jeremy's door, the hinge here was silent—oiled—and as I'd suspected, the door to the outside was just beyond the entryway. A pool scoop stood against the jamb, a long metal pole with a plastic rectangle on top, mesh stretched inside it.

Like it had been put there just for me.

I punched my hand through the mesh, then adjusted the metal pole to its shortest setting—snug beneath my arm, enough to pinch my armpit when I leaned on it for support, but it would work. If I hurried.

Outside, the driving rain attacked with renewed ferocity as I stepped onto the stamped concrete—slippery and shiny as glass even in the hazy dawn. The aluminum base of my makeshift crutch slid against the cement with a harsh grinding sound, and the wrought iron gate squeaked in a way that I felt more than heard. And here the tricky part; I'd have to sneak past the kitchen window to get to the driveway. I sidled up as close to the house as I could, listened for two frantic heartbeats, and booked it, ducking beneath the kitchen window at a halting, uneven run, biting my lip against the throb in my ankle. I nearly tripped over the electrical box, but I managed to catch myself on the brick. I had pulled one of the lines loose, though—a thin gray cord. The phone line? They didn't need that anyway.

The driveway was slicker than the stamped concrete of the pool, years of dripping engine oil, the remnants of gasoline and tire debris greasing the road. The rubber base of the aluminum pole skidded from beneath me, and I flailed for a moment, then steadied. If they looked out the window now, they'd be able to see me, though they'd have to press their faces close to the glass and peer to their left. But if I could make it to the trees...

Three steps, four. The emerald lawn squelched beneath my shoes, but the grass provided purchase for my good foot, and the aluminum pole sank into the earth enough to let me more or less pole vault across the yard to the tree line.

Even here I sensed—hopefully imaginary—eyes boring a hole in my back. No one could see me here, I didn't think. Still, I waited a moment, listening for the slamming of a door, for someone to call my name through the rain, but the only noises were the moaning breath of wind and the hiss of raging water.

I squinted through the gloom, much darker beneath the trees. It seemed someone—Cherie or Preston or even Jeremy—had made a thin trail through the woods parallel to the driveway; despite the rain, I could see the deep ruts in the earth. Bike tires? Ah, they hadn't cut the trail out, they'd ridden it down to the ground. I soon understood why. The drive went up over a hill and then slipped down at an extreme angle; in the dirt, a mountain bike would have more control over speed and direction.

The wind howled more loudly the farther I got from the house, screaming in my ears, drops stinging the back of my neck, rainwater washing salt into my ears and mouth. My eyes burned. My ankle burned more, every lurching step leading to a fresh round of throbbing. I kept going. And going.

Preston had said the drive was a mile long. I had hoped that was hyperbole, but it appeared he was telling the truth. Figured.

And then I heard it—the rushing of water. I hobbled over a final set of brambles and almost tripped straight down the ravine, but the aluminum pole, sticking securely in the mud along the side of the bike path, kept me upright. I clung to the slick metal and peered down the embankment.

The ground here sloped steeply down to the river, which was swollen with rainwater and capped in white wind-whipped swells. From the edge, I could see the bridge Preston had mentioned—much larger than I had imagined. Not just a bridge, but a covered bridge, the kind you saw in old westerns, wide enough for wagons and horses. Pillars of cement sank into the earth on both shores, rebar supporting the structure from beneath. And it wasn't only a tree that blocked our way out. The bridge itself was intact most of the way across, the pillars holding strong, but the wooden boards on the side nearest the driveway had collapsed—a space far too wide to jump a car across. That's why Dad wasn't bothering with the tree: cutting it aside wouldn't matter if we still couldn't drive over the bridge. Waiting out the storm then carrying me back through the woods to our truck was the fastest option.

But... the bridge...

I frowned. The maple that had fallen was not a monster. Through the barrage of branches and leaves, I could see where it had split, down the embankment on the other side of the drive. At the base, it was no bigger than four feet across. With the cement reinforcements, the bridge should have held.

I hauled myself away from the edge and across the asphalt driveway, grinding my teeth in time to the rhythmic stabbing of my ankle bone. I was making it worse, but I had all the time in the world to heal. Provided we got out of this place. And I wasn't naive enough to assume that was a given.

I used the pole to drag myself over the thick branches on the other side of the driveway, but the picker vines snagged it incessantly, snarling my makeshift crutch in greedy fingers of thorn. When I almost stumbled to the earth again, I abandoned the crutch against a prickly evergreen bush. The relief in my armpit was palpable, but my ankle throbbed. Dammit. Why did everything have to be so hard?

Then again, no treasure hunt was worth doing if it was easy.

Another downed tree blocked my path to the embankment, but the trunk was low enough to get over. I sat on the tree, the rough bark chafing my butt, then rolled my legs to the other side and lowered my feet into the marshy dirt. Electricity shot though my ankle, then straight up my spine into my head—the brittle shock of it flared deep in the roots of my teeth.

I moaned. And lowered my butt to the ground.

What are you doing, Poppy?

What has to be done, that's what.

I scooted toward the embankment. Rocks and brush, probably more than a few rattlesnakes, but I didn't think they'd bother attacking me—the river was swollen enough to chase most wildlife to higher ground. I carefully eased down over the large stones nearest the drive, then slipped lower, using my good foot to crab-walk and shimmy, holding my bad ankle as high as I could.

And then I was on the shore not three feet from the fallen tree. The stones were slippery here, the ground marshy with the rising water. Every step sucked at my shoes, loosing the subtle musty scent of river muck and wet silt.

But— *Huh*. The tree was not split as it had appeared from the other side. I ran my fingers over the indentations on the trunk, uniform and circular. From a chainsaw, definitely from a chainsaw, but these were not marks from someone trying to free the tree from blocking the drive—the striations also cut the trunk where the tree had obviously snapped. And what was missing was more suspicious: the maple was not marred by blackened wood. There were no jagged slashes from an electrical pulse.

I peered up at the underside of the bridge. Eight feet away, but I recognized the chainsaw markings there too.

This wasn't lightning.

It also wasn't a mistake.

Preston had vandalized the bridge and cut the tree down to cover it up. Some children might have suspected my father—he was gone when I awoke the night I heard the saw—but Dad hadn't brought a chainsaw with us, and he'd returned to me within ten minutes of my hearing the blade. No way possible he could have walked here, cut up the tree, and made it back in time. Plus, he had absolutely zero motive to do this.

But Preston did.

Preston had an escape plan, too—a bag of money.

Maybe he had a car parked a mile up the road. Maybe he had another secret bag of cash, or he'd cleaned out their surely massive bank accounts. Had I missed something in his office?

Either way, he had blocked the drive on purpose, and Cherie would have noticed—eventually. She would have known he had tried to trap her here. There was no logical reason for him to do this unless he was planning to get rid of his wife altogether, either because she knew too much about his misdeeds or because he didn't want to share his money in a divorce.

I wondered how long Cherie would have made it if we hadn't appeared outside her door.

And what would he do to us? We'd stumbled into something far more sinister than domestic violence, more sinister still than a child abuser trying to hide his crimes. Preston couldn't just let us go, not now. You could never let outsiders know who you were—who you really were. Even if we only knew about the abuse, about the money, about the tree... we still knew far too much.

CHAPTER FOURTEEN

THE RETURN TRIP was significantly harder—all uphill. My thighs burned, my ankle screamed, my lungs were tight with exertion.

Even then I didn't panic. There was always a chance I wouldn't live to see tomorrow, and every day was a step closer to death. They called that existential depression, but maybe the truth was just depressing, and it certainly didn't mean something was wrong with me for recognizing that.

Besides, my father would protect me, I knew that with the pure certainty that only children possess. But he had to know what to protect me from; I needed to tell my father what I'd discovered, even if I only had a few pieces to the puzzle. I didn't have proof that Preston had hurt his son, but I had evidence that he'd trapped his wife here—trapped us here too. That he had a hidden bag of money. I certainly had enough to know that I wanted to leave this house immediately, storm or not.

I lurched back over the lawn and under the window and in through the pool house door—sneaky and silent.

I had to get cleaned up before I wandered into the

kitchen. What if Preston was in there now? If he saw me soaked like this, it wouldn't take a genius to figure out where I'd been. And once he knew I was on to him, well...

I could grab a towel from the pool house, then head back to Jeremy's room and dry off enough to avoid much scrutiny, depending on how long they let me "sleep." I had planned my morning well, even if I hadn't anticipated the wet trek to the bridge.

My shoes squelched against the tiles.

Just inside the pool house door was another short hallway, a single door on the left side. I pushed it open on the way past—a closet. Shelves of sunscreen, a hanging rack of deflated pool toys, a Donatello float front and center. The boy's favorite? Was this room, like the bedroom, another off-limits space? But even if this closet held memories, it did not hold towels.

I closed the closet door behind me.

At the end of the short hallway, the space opened up into what resembled a locker room, but not any kind of locker room I'd ever been in. A locker room in a school where parents didn't have a better place to spend all those extra dollars—people too privileged to understand what poverty looked like, what it might be like for one man to fund an entire school. The tiles were brilliant white with a vein of turquoise stone running through them. Two parallel shower heads poked from the wall behind floor-to-ceiling glass, more of that marble tile covering the walls. And... it smelled. Not of chlorine and other pool chemicals—metallic. Rusting pipes from the unused shower heads? The stink from the broken toilet?

Another door waited on the far side of the room, probably where the defunct commode was hiding. *Come on—this place is a stupid maze.* I could see a niche around the other side of the shower stalls; if the towels weren't there, I'd go back to the bedroom and use a blanket to dry my hair. Maybe one of Jeremy's T-shirts because his parents made dumb decisions regarding linens.

I stepped forward, wincing, then realized the area wasn't just a niche. It was an open room.

My breath froze in my lungs. The window on the far wall showed the kidney-shaped pool outdoors, the turquoise water dangerously close to overflowing. In front of that window, a hot tub had been built into the floor, two steps leading up to it.

And it wasn't empty.

Preston reclined in the tub, one of his arms resting on the side beyond his stocky frame—relaxing, or hiding his face after what he'd done to Cherie.

No, no, no. To come all this way and get busted now... it wasn't fair. Preston wasn't looking my way, but he had to have heard the door open. What was he waiting for? Why wasn't he threatened by my presence? Unless everyone else was already dead. Maybe he'd killed my dad because I hadn't warned him.

That thought stopped my heart, but a growl of thunder started it back up again. Ridiculous—children often were. My father was much smarter than Preston, and surely more cautious; he'd never let this man get the better of him. But why was he so still? Even if Preston hadn't heard the door... he should have moved by now.

I limped nearer, extra careful on the slick marble. Were the tiles near the tub... stained? Yes. A sickly watered-down pink. My feet moved, my ankle forgotten, the hot tub sidling nearer, nearer until I could see into the water. Until I could see his face.

One of his cheekbones was dark, the line clearly

defined, a single blow with a heavy object. His eyes were wide to the ceiling—unseeing. Blank. The water was murky, too dark to see much more than the vague outline of dead flesh beneath the surface. Then I remembered—the flashlight.

I slid it from my pocket and clicked it on, the water glittering a garish pinkish-red. On the arm beneath the water, a deep slash split the skin from his wrist to the middle of his forearm.

Had he felt guilty about beating Cherie and slit his wrist? That seemed unlikely. Had he realized he was trapped—that he'd go to jail for hurting his wife in front of us? And where was the blade? If he'd killed himself, no one would take the weapon. Looking back, I think I was still holding on to some childhood notion of hope, though I'm not sure what I was hoping for. Maybe hope that there was still something to save Cherie from. With Preston gone, she didn't need us—didn't need me. It was a bit out of character for me to see myself as anyone's savior, but humans are rarely as consistent as they believe. Under the right circumstances, a person is capable of anything, whether it be dastardly or heroic, and the lines between are not always clearly drawn.

I leaned over the bloody water, shining the light on his feet, the edges of his toes. His hairy legs. His penis, limp against his thigh. I looked a few extra moments at that, I can admit it now. I don't think I'd ever seen a penis in real life, and I didn't suppose he'd mind.

When I was done getting an eyeful—less than an eyeful, let's be honest—I struggled up the last step. The blade lay beneath his hip after all, near his hand, fingers as limp as his penis.

Yet my gaze was locked on something else. I'd only ever

seen him wearing a raincoat or a cloak of shadows; now I noticed a crude outline on the back of Preston's elbow, navy blue and faded as if it had been sketched in pen. A prison tattoo. Of a sea turtle.

And that turtle exactly matched the watermark on my pen pal's stationery.

I stumbled back off the Jacuzzi steps. Preston was a bad man, a man who'd traumatized his own child, who had a bag of cash as an escape plan. He was also the one I'd been writing to every other week for months.

But that wasn't the part squeezing my lungs.

My father had brought us to these woods, to this mountain. And that was no coincidence.

My father *knew*.

Familiar idioms—*in the soup, borrowing trouble*—didn't prove anything. And Preston being dead didn't prove he was my pen pal. But I felt it in my guts, and my father taught me to listen to that.

You feel things like broken flower stems before you see them. You feel the danger before you understand.

CHAPTER FIFTEEN

THIS IS the part of the story where people start yelling things like "The killer was in the house the whole time!" Of course they're right, but the most terrifying of killers would never do something so tacky as call people to warn them. Those killers prefer the messiness: the tearful shock on their victims' faces, the way bodily fluids go tacky on their fingers. At least I assume that's the draw. All this time, and I've never asked my father why. Guessing is more interesting than whatever the truth might be, and probably a lot more comforting.

I'm not sure how long I stood beside the tub with my shoulder against the wall, the smell of blood stinging my nostrils. Rain sheeted down the windows like a waterfall, the kind of waterfall I should have been visiting that weekend—the kind of waterfall my father said I fell off of. It made me feel like we were in a bubble where the rest of the world didn't exist.

Inside a bubble with a dead man who had been writing me letters for months. I was locked inside a bubble with the person who'd killed him.

But not everything made sense. Yes, my father had a reason to bring me to this house—he knew who my pen pal was, and he'd come here to teach Preston a lesson about respecting little girls. But my father wasn't the one who'd cut down the tree across the bridge. Had he somehow known what Preston was planning and figured he could help Cherie? That seemed possible—having a rich woman in his debt was highly pragmatic. And my father was a researcher; he knew everything about everyone, and he'd certainly take the time to look into the person who was writing me.

But if Dad knew who Preston was, then why would he let the man knock on my door when he wasn't around to protect me? My father would never put me in harm's way. And Dad could have come here on his own; he didn't have to drag me out into the forest. And what was he going to do before I accidentally hurt my ankle, walk up and punch Preston in the face?

That wasn't my father's style. Another man, maybe. A less controlled man. But not my dad.

I left the pool scoop in the closet with the inflatables. No one would notice a broken pool net. No one would care.

We would have to go back to the campsite for our things, I realized. We couldn't just leave our tent in the woods so close to the crime scene. And that's all this giant home was now: a crime scene.

I made my way to the door and back out into the driving rain. I'm not sure why I didn't just walk into the kitchen—the threat was gone, right? At least the threat to me. But Cherie didn't know about the tree, I didn't think. Cherie would wonder about my wet hair. She'd ask questions. I blinked, and behind my eyelids I saw the body in the tub—a pedophile. A man who deserved it, who'd wanted to hurt me, who had already hurt his family. But my gut clenched anyway.

I didn't want Cherie asking questions, didn't want her to see Preston in that tub. For a few hours, even a day, she would be safe. She'd be safe until she realized she was witness to a murder.

And what then? Nothing good. Leaving witnesses was irrational—unacceptable. Witnesses didn't get to walk away. I'd known as much when I thought Preston was the culprit; I was positive now that I knew it was my father.

I barely felt the cold as I limped across the pool's deck toward the back of the house where Jeremy's window was.

How long would it take Cherie to realize her husband was gone—really gone? I thought maybe she wouldn't mind. Maybe she'd be... happy.

Hope. It's so foolish.

I stumbled through the gardens along the back side of the house. My ankle ached, a brighter throbbing now that seemed to spike in time to the flashes of lightning that veined the clouds. The painkillers Cherie had given me the night before had processed out of my system, presumably returning the pain to its baseline state—horrendous. Unless I'd hurt my ankle worse when I went traipsing down to the bridge, inflamed the tendons or something. That was a distinct possibility.

I tugged the edge of the screen's frame, and the entire insert popped with a *thwong*. The window beyond was trickier with the slick glass; it took three tries for me to suction my palms to the pane. I knew it wasn't locked, though—I'd taken care of that before I left the house. It was my plan B. My "in case." Dad always said you should have an "in case."

Yet, my heart still leaped when the window ground

upward. I groaned as I hauled myself up the brick, the window ledge grating against my ribs, my belly. Walking my hands over Jeremy's desk was tricky, and I cried out when I hit my ankle on the windowsill, but then I was on the floor, panting. *Almost there, Poppy. You can do this.*

The window squeaked closed. Nothing I could do about the screen, but that wouldn't matter—there were far more pressing issues here than screens. I stripped and rubbed the bedsheet over my wet skin and used it to dry my hair. I tugged a sundress then a sweatshirt over my head, over the fresh scratches that covered my ribs, every movement making my leg hurt worse than it had the moment before.

From the main room came the clattering of silverware on the marble table. I could hear the low murmur of voices too—my father for sure. And Cherie. I was running out of time.

But how to play this? What was my strategy? Maybe I should stay here, pretend to be asleep until I figured it out, or—

"Poppy!" my father called. "Breakfast!"

Time's up. I paused at the closed door, then carefully peeked into the hallway—empty save for that thin table with its elaborately painted vase, the glass shiny with lacquer. Brilliantly green even in the gloom.

My father and Cherie both looked up from their seats at the table as I shuffled through the main living area, using the piano as a crutch and then the end table. They made no move to help me—they knew I was old enough to do it on my own. Hurt but not broken. Practically an adult. And it was time that I started acting like it.

Cherie smiled and scooped eggs onto my already-set plate, then settled back in her seat. "Glad we have a gas stove." There was a bowl of fruit salad, too, and another plate of croissants. Did she always have an enormous stockpile of pastries? Rich people were weird. Dad and I had money, but we didn't live beyond the means of most people in town. We were comfortable, and that was all. That was enough.

I might have been wincing, because she said, "You poor dear. Does it hurt worse today?"

I shook my head and made sure my face was even—like a grown-up. "Not worse. But it certainly isn't healed." I chuckled—*no big deal, just an ankle, right?*—but it did hurt. A lot. My heart was beating in my toes.

My father narrowed his eyes. "I assume you have more Tylenol, Cherie?" He knew—he always knew—and though he was talking to Cherie, he was looking straight at me. Wondering about my damp hair? Cherie hadn't even noticed.

But she should have picked up on her husband's absence. Time was running out on that too—once she found Preston, it was over.

I didn't want it to be over. I wasn't ready to go home—back to all the kids who acted like I did not exist. Here, I was real to everyone. Well, everyone who was still breathing.

Cherie nodded, then patted my arm as if we'd known each other forever. Like a mother would. Looking back, I think I wanted to pretend a little longer. The reality of having a mother never worked out, but for a day... it was nice.

I blinked at my dad, his gaze still on me. I forced a smile. "I'm having a good time here, Dad. I should slide off waterfalls more often. I almost don't want the storm to end." I was asking him, practically begging him, if we could stay. A few hours, a day, even two where we could be a normal family in a world apart from ours. Would he think it was stupid? Irrational? Emotional? My breath was icy in my lungs.

He stared for another frantic heartbeat, then let one corner of his mouth turn up. *Okay, Poppy. Okay.*

Cherie laughed; my father chuckled too. Then he finally released my gaze and went back to his food.

I turned back to my plate, too, but my stomach had soured, a strange mix of relief and dread. That day, just for a day, I could know what it was to have a mom. Today, I could protect her.

But soon, she'd be gone.

Unless I could find a way to save her for good.

CHAPTER SIXTEEN

I FINISHED my eggs and let Cherie lead me to the piano, my father vanishing out the front door with a backward wave. The tree—he had to clear the tree, he said. But that wasn't what he was doing. Luckily, Cherie didn't seem to know that.

Cherie lowered herself onto the piano bench beside me. The room was clouded in the hazy brown dimness common in log homes, the weakened hint of cloud-marred sun bouncing against the wooden beams and reflecting back a muddy light that made the room appear warmer.

Not that it needed to be warmer. Sweat prickled along the back of my neck. The only thing keeping me cool was the breeze that whispered against my shins and up my thighs. I never wore skirts at home. It felt like being naked.

"This way," Cherie said, and gently guided my hands to the piano. She rested hers on the keys an octave above mine and pressed one ivory rectangle with her middle finger. "This is a C. Follow me."

I did. *C-C, E-E, A-A, C-C, F-F, A-A, G-G, B-B...* Her practiced movements were not enough to drag my attention from the thoughts inside my brain, but it was hard to forget a dead body and the impending demise of the kind woman who had tended your wounds.

"Great job, Poppy. You can hold the notes, or you can make them more staccato, like this." She demonstrated.

I kept going, playing an actual melody. I had never considered playing an instrument. Other children did it for the fun of it, adults, too, but my father never even listened to music in the house. He didn't sing songs. The fairies were our one eccentricity. Our one fanciful thing.

The weird thing that made us more real.

But, oh, to watch Cherie play, the balls of her cheeks high and pink with the joy of it... it was strange. Disconcerting, if I had to guess now, but at the time, I let it consume me until I was no longer focused on the dead man. I no longer thought about how she'd be gone soon, too. How all I wanted to do was save her, and I couldn't. Could I? Maybe... But no, definitely not.

I smiled—she was nice, she deserved that—while she played a different part of the song, a pretty tinkling above my still-moving hands, a melody that she matched to my sometimes clumsy plucking. A duet.

And though I knew the answer, I couldn't stop thinking: *She doesn't have to know about the bathroom. Can we take her home with us?* Like she was a puppy. A thing to be fed and taken for walks and put down when she got to be too much trouble.

But no vanilla mom would willingly leave a place like this to move in with a murderer. Money could buy a lot of things even if people didn't like to admit it; money could buy love, it could buy trust, and damn near anything else. What money couldn't do was force you to forget that the man you lived with was a killer.

Then again... she had already been living with a monster.

Her fingers kept on going, playing, playing, playing, and I followed along—*C-C, E-E*... We played so long that my fingers cramped. But the pills were helping. My ankle throbbed less and less as the minutes ticked past, and by the time we stopped playing, the pain had faded to a hazy tightness around my foot.

My brain was foggy too—dizzy when I moved my head. Tired? Or the pain. Or... stress.

"Do you think my dad will be back soon?" I asked. I wanted to talk to him. I wanted to know what we were going to do—what the plan was. Could I convince him that Cherie should live with us? Would he think it was a stupid idea? Of course he would.

"He's working on that tree with Preston. I'm sure they'll be in soon."

No they won't. And no one was working on the tree. Dad might be moving Preston's body, positioning the corpse so the animals would take care of the carcass, destroying any evidence... or making it look like a hunting accident. If he did that, maybe Cherie would be okay—she never had to know it was murder. Perhaps my father had never intended to hurt her at all.

I frowned at the sheet music stand. My reflection peered back, translucent in the shiny black surface, all the more visible because the light behind me had brightened. The clouds were still heavy, the rain still pounding, but it was not nearly as dark now. The storm was letting up.

"Yeah, I'm sure you're right." I forced a smile. "I just didn't hear the chainsaw."

She pushed herself to her feet and patted my shoulder,

reassuring and gentle. "We don't own a chainsaw, dear. But those hand axes should do the trick."

I might have believed it, if I were a different child.

But when we first got there, she'd told Preston to grab the chainsaw to clear the driveway.

I'd heard her.

CHAPTER SEVENTEEN

I LEFT Cherie with the same kind of backward wave my dad had given us on his way out the door, then limped back to the bedroom—more an awkward half-stumble and not only because of my leg. I felt off-balance, like I wanted to throw up. I needed a minute to myself.

Jeremy's door opened—silent. I frowned. Had the hinge fixed itself? No, that didn't make sense, that was suspicious, that was—

"It seems we should have a conversation."

I jumped, smashing my elbow into the knob with enough force to slam the door closed and send an electric jolt of pain from my elbow to my shoulder. Not to be outdone, my ankle responded with a burst of renewed throbbing.

My father walked out of the shadows at the back of the room and leaned his hip against Jeremy's desk. "You saw him." Not a question.

Bile rose in my gorge—nauseated. So dizzy. Now that the adrenaline had waned, the day was catching up to me, trying to tug me to the carpet. "There's money. Under the mattress."

One corner of his mouth turned up, pleased but not surprised. "Good. That's better than there not being money under the mattress."

I swallowed hard. "Did you put him in the woods or something? Is that where you were?" When he raised an eyebrow, I went on: "Cherie... she seems nice. And she didn't deserve what he did to her, and he might have hurt their son too. Maybe she won't be upset that he's dead, especially if she thinks it was an accident. Or she could come home with us just to make sure." *To make sure she's not a risk if she stays alive.* I was rambling, my words pressured and tight.

He frowned—actual surprise this time, something I rarely saw in him, but I never really asked him for anything either. And what I wanted to ask for... well. It was a big risk. It was impossible. And I knew it.

So when he cleared his throat, the temperature in the room dropped. "Do you think she *should* come home with us?" His voice was cold, each word slow and deliberate.

"Probably not," I said, just as slowly, my gaze drifting beyond him, to the window. The screen—he'd put it back in. Because to leave it out was a mistake. My heart sank. I shouldn't ask for anything else, but my mouth kept forming words: "Maybe she could stay for a few weeks; you could feel her out. She said she was going to teach me how to play piano."

"You believed her?"

"She already taught me scales. And this pretty duet..."

He pushed himself off the desk—he seemed taller than usual, but that might have been the too-tight T-shirt. "She killed her husband, Poppy. Do you think she's a safe person to invite into our home?"

I blinked. *Cherie* killed her husband?

"To be fair, I think it was an accident—they were fighting. But her boy died under suspicious circumstances, too, so I believe she had a lot of reasons to get rid of him. Children rarely fall off mountains, and waterfalls even less frequently."

Fall off... that was why he'd told them I fell off a waterfall? It was a... taunt?

"If anything ever happened to you, Poppy, I'd never forgive myself."

I already knew that. And I knew about the boy—that Preston had hurt him. But Cherie? Vanilla Cherie? No, this was all wrong. *Preston was my pen pal. You came here for him, didn't you, Dad? He was writing me letters—he was dangerous.* My brain was dizzy and foggy and spun with unanswered questions. Bile burned the base of my esophagus.

But... maybe it wasn't so far-fetched. I had heard Cherie and Preston fighting—only Cherie and Preston. I'd heard the clatter of something being thrown. I blinked now, and behind my eyelids, I could see the injury on Preston's dead face—the bruising. I think that was what convinced me.

Normal people led with their emotions. They were irrational, illogical. They punched and fought and screamed. Dad didn't punch—he had his blade. He didn't fight because he didn't have to; didn't have a single defensive wound on him either, unlike Cherie. And he never lied, not to me. In a house like ours, there were a lot of things you could get away with, but if we weren't honest with each other, we were screwed. I had to know the truth—he had to tell me or I might say something wrong. And he was telling me that...

Cherie. Cherie had killed her husband.

There was one thing I needed him to confirm, even if I already knew the answer. "We came here on purpose. Didn't we, Dad?"

He nodded. "Ah, my Poppy. So smart—wicked sharp." That phrase again. Strangely, I don't ever remember him using it after that trip. Looking back now, those days in the mountains existed in a place outside our reality. Three days where our normal no longer endured. Where anything felt possible.

My father stepped closer. "Cherie isn't a good fit for us, Poppy. Not for the long-term."

"She might be!" The words exploded from my lips before I could stop them. How could he be so sure?

He shook his head. "You remember what I said, don't you? About the butterflies? About people?"

"Yes, Dad." That people were fragile—that they had to choose us. But she couldn't come to that decision because she feared we'd tell the police she'd killed her husband. Fear waned; loyalty stuck. If she wanted us, she'd have to prove it.

"Do you really want her to be your mother, Poppy?"

My mother. I'd been thinking it since the first time those words left his lips, maybe from the first time I saw her, but it felt like a trick question now. A smart person would not say yes to that, not so easily. And we'd need to figure out so much—would she come live with us? How would they explain Preston? Instead of asking those questions, I shrugged. "Does she love you?" If she loved him, if she proved it... it could work. Would we be having this discussion if it couldn't work?

"Does she love me?" He chuckled. "You tell me." I heard what he was saying: *test her*. He was giving me the decision—even if he didn't agree, even if he didn't think she should come with us... he was trusting me. I'd never felt more grown-up, but my belly was sour and sick, my lungs so tight it was hard to draw breath.

He met my eyes. "You're a responsible young woman, Poppy. I'll let you decide. But you need to make that choice today. We can't stay here forever."

It didn't occur to me then that it was a test I was doomed to fail.

But it should have.

CHAPTER EIGHTEEN

"I'm going to help Cherie with the dishes," he said. "Do you want to lie down before lunch?"

Yes. I should have been poking at her, asking questions, coming up with some effective way to test whether she'd fit with us, but my eyes were full of sand—my joints ached. The night spent pondering the money beneath Jeremy's bed and the morning spent struggling through brush to investigate that tree had sapped my energy. But mostly, I needed to be off my ankle. Though Cherie had given me more medication to take the edge off, it was swelling again. The steady pulsing of my heart had intensified, ripping through the marrow of my shin in ever more excruciating beats.

I let my father cover me with the fleece blanket—we tossed the wet sheet in the corner—and settled back against the pillows, my eyes closed against the hazy light that leaked in through the window. Cherie had killed her husband. In this house, she was the murderer. Not Dad. And this was disquieting. My father wouldn't hurt me, but how certain was I about Cherie? Cherie had lied to me about the chainsaw. Cherie had smiled at me, knowing her abusive husband was already dead—her husband who was a pedophile, who might have killed their child. I was sure her relief was normal, even a certain giddiness at revenge taken against the man who'd hurt her, but the devil you knew was always better than the one you didn't. And my father... he didn't think she fit. Was he wrong? Doubting him made me sick to my stomach. He always knew what was right—he could read people much better than I could.

When I opened my eyes again, the room was dark. And Cherie was screaming.

Oh no. I shot to seated, my heart a pulsing, choking pressure in my throat, dizziness tugging me back to the mattress. I'd slept the entire day—how had I done that? And Dad... he'd said I only had the day to make this choice. Had he made it for me?

I practically leaped from the bed, still woozy, trying not to puke, but though I could handle the nausea, I couldn't deal as efficiently with the pain. The moment my ankle hit the floor, sweet agony exploded in my brain, and I collapsed back against the bed, gingerly rubbing at my shin. Cherie screamed again.

No, no, no. It wasn't supposed to happen this fast! I ground my teeth and forced myself up.

The screaming was louder in the hallway. Coming from down the hall—her bedroom?

I stumbled, caught myself on the wall, and felt my way along through the blackness. No, not her bedroom—too close. The spare: my father's room. She shrieked, a single loud bleat of pain. This wasn't fair. Not at all. He'd *promised.*

Though... he might've had a reason. Maybe she'd freaked out on him—tried to hurt him the way she'd hurt Preston.

The screaming stopped suddenly. Was she dead? I paused outside the door, my hand on the knob.

I'm not sure what I thought about while I stood there. The rain was pounding again, attacking the windows, I remember that much—like thousands of stones hammering the roof. I couldn't hear her, not anymore; couldn't hear anything except the storm. I guess I wanted to know if she was gone. I wanted to know if it was over. Once things were over, you had to let them go. There was no choice; there was no more pressure either, but I don't think I cared about that when I turned the knob.

I squinted through the crack.

My father's room wasn't as elaborately decorated as Jeremy's, just a single dresser topped with a mirror on the wall in front of me. The mirror was the reason I could see the bed—well, that and the flickering yellow glow from the candles. My foot throbbed in time to my heartbeat.

My father was on top of her, his hands around her throat. And he was naked, his ass pulsing in the mirror. Was she dead? Was he... *doing it* with a dead woman?

Kids are pretty clear that they don't want to see their parents doing it, but most don't have to know the sheer horror of thinking they might be watching their father have sex with a dead body.

But then one of her arms flew up, her hand a claw, gripping his bicep; my shoulders relaxed. *She's not dead.* He was still strangling her, though—just because she was fighting didn't mean she'd live. But...

He raised his hands from her throat, and the intake of breath that exploded from her lips was louder than the storm, a great heaving inhale. And then... she screamed again. I startled, gasped—*shit!*—then clasped my hands over my mouth to cover the sound.

I had been wrong. Those were not cries of pain.

My father snaked his elbow under her knee and yanked it up onto his shoulder. She screamed louder, their image in the mirror vibrating—shaking the bed.

I slunk back into the hallway and leaned against the doorjamb. He wasn't having sex with a dead body, and he wasn't assaulting her either; it would have been easier for me to believe that he was having sex with a corpse than that he would rape a woman.

As if to emphasize the point, his voice filtered out into the hall. "Smile for me," he growled. "I want to know I make you happy."

Ewwwww. Gross. Was that how people talked during sex? I recognized the timbre—that was Dad's charmer voice. He used it at school, and at town hall meetings. At barbecues. I hoped I didn't envision him doing this the next time he used that voice with the reverend. Spoiler: I did.

"I have a feeling I'll be smiling from here on out," she breathed. Her voice was hoarse, probably because she liked being strangled. *So weird.* Dad didn't have normal hobbies, but his motivation to live and protect his offspring were always in line with what I thought people should want—evolution, right? It made logical sense. Normal people playing at death seemed infinitely more distressing.

"I've been waiting for this for so long." Cherie moaned, a low hiss—definitely pleasure. How stupid that I had thought differently. But I'd had no reason before then to think they were... together.

I knew I'd stumbled onto some divine truth—a plot. A secret. And... not necessarily a bad one.

Was he stacking the deck because he knew that I wanted a mother? This made absolute and complete sense to me then—makes sense to me now too. He'd have given me whatever I wanted so long as he could do it safely. But it took a certain kind of woman to be with my father. My biological mom never wanted to be a parent; she liked her drugs more than her baby. Sharon hadn't been able to handle living with us—she was weak. But... maybe Cherie could handle him. Could handle me.

Cherie moaned again, and it echoed against the walls and inside my head.

If I had to guess, looking back, I'd say that this was the moment I really thought it might be possible. This woman had enough of her own secrets that it just might work between them. But the way she was talking, *waiting for this for so long...* It was as if they'd known one another for years. That part didn't make sense. Unless she really wanted sex and hadn't seen a penis—any penis—for a long time, though I couldn't see what would be so great about the act itself. Even now, I don't understand that level of craving. You don't even need two good hands these days, just batteries.

The room spun. I hobbled around the edge of the rug, toward Jeremy's bedroom, but I'd forgotten about the hall table.

My foot caught on the leg of the table, and I went sprawling, the green vase flying—everything gray in the hazy darkness. It smashed against the hardwood with a dense thunk. Stars flashed behind my eyelids, and lightning exploded in my ankle bone, a power surge of agony. I cried out, a high whining noise—pathetic—and blinked, trying to breathe, but the air was dusty and dry, sending me into a coughing spasm. What the heck? Something thick and powdery in the air. I could feel it in my nostrils. There was grit in my mouth, caught in my teeth—sandpaper on my tongue. I sneezed.

Ashes. Oh god, they were ashes. Jeremy's? *Oh no.*

The moaning in Dad's room had stopped.

I rolled onto my good knee and spread my arms, trying to sweep the dust, *her child*, into a pile. If this woman might come home with us—if we needed her to *choose* to come home with us—I certainly didn't want her to think there was something wrong with me. An unwanted child could be too much pressure—it could break a woman. And then I'd have to let her go.

"Poppy?"

A light flickered through the powdery haze, and then Cherie crystalized, haloed in the yellowed glow of the candle. At least she'd put on a robe. I didn't want to think about her being naked. I'd seen quite enough already.

"Are you okay, sweetheart?" She righted the table and lowered the candle onto it, then knelt at my side.

"I'm fine. I'm so, so sorry." My voice quavered—my ankle really hurt. I coughed again, but this time it stuck around, a long raspy fit of hacking and sputtering.

"It's okay, honey." She offered me a hand. "Let's get you back to bed, and I'll take care of this." But unlike my shaking voice, hers had a hard edge to it. She was only pretending it was okay.

Mad about the vase? About the dust that used to be her son? And what now? Could we... vacuum up a child?

My father leaned against the doorframe and crossed his arms—wearing shorts, thank god he was wearing shorts. But he wasn't watching me. Watching Cherie, his... girlfriend? Sex didn't mean you were bonded for life, but I liked the way it sounded: *girlfriend*.

"We should get cleaned up, then we can all get to know one another a little better," he said to Cherie.

My face heated. *Get to know one another*—that's what he'd said, but I knew what he was telling me: he was providing me the opportunity I'd missed while I was asleep. I'd have a chance to ask questions, a chance to test her, a chance… to make a decision about her. The right decision.

I nodded dumbly, feeling three steps behind already. It was stupid, I guess, sitting in that cloud of little-boy dust, looking at her. But I couldn't pull my gaze away from her face, the subtle swelling along her jaw, her eyes glittering with some emotion I could not identify—in the throes of passion less than a day after killing her husband.

I'd pegged Preston as screwed up from the moment he walked into the house.

I never suspected Cherie at all.

CHAPTER NINETEEN

"If I didn't know better, I'd think you were letting me win." Cherie's face shimmered, animated in the candle she'd settled on the marble tabletop. The living room appeared larger in the dark.

I wasn't sure what time it was. After waking up to the weird sex stuff in the bedroom and spilling Cherie's son on the ground, I'd lost all sense of the hours. I wasn't even sure why we were playing cards, though I doubt it would have mattered exactly what we were doing. All that mattered was making this decision.

And I'd wasted an entire day in bed already.

"I'm not trying to let you win. I'm bad at this game," I said. I wasn't—it was easy—but this wasn't the time to act high-and-mighty. I collected my cards. Three-handed Euchre, the only game both my father and Cherie knew. Later, I'd find out that the game was not popular in the south. Spades, Hearts... but not Euchre. I should have found it strange that both of them knew the rules, being staunch southerners and all, but I had more important things to consider, like how to show my father that Cherie would be good for us. And how I could get her to prove it. I couldn't just say yes to such a significant life change—my father was a pragmatic man, and I needed logical reasoning behind my choice.

"How do you feel about Alabama?" I asked. That seemed like a good starter question.

Cherie smiled and glanced from her cards to my face. "I hear it's lovely. Not as many mountains down there as there are up here, but I could sell this place. Start over." She drew her gaze to my father and winked, then laid a card on the tabletop: the queen of hearts.

I watched Cherie as I had in the hallway, on the lookout for surprise or even trepidation, but she only smiled. It wasn't a shock that my father had been able to seduce her—sex was a thing some people did for comfort. But to get her to... leave her mansion and move away with us? Had he convinced her that she had to run after killing Preston? That he'd hide her—protect her? That made sense. But it all seemed so... easy.

My father's eyes were on me, steady—he was waiting for me to act. He hadn't even played his card.

My heart sank. *Think, Poppy, think.* It was a test, as much of me as of her. I studied her face, the way she batted her eyes at my dad, trying to see what he saw.

She wasn't a psychopath, despite her muted response to Preston's death. Hers was a different kind of numbness, how you walled yourself off when you'd lost hope. Had it been born of grief after the loss of her son, or was it born of desperation from her current predicament? Was this what my father saw too? Did he think that numbness would make her a bad mother, therefore not a good match long-term?

"Did you love your son?" I asked.

My father narrowed his eyes and played the nine of

hearts. I tossed the king. My trick—our trick. I collected the cards and played the ace of clubs.

"I loved Jeremy more than I could ever say." That was the right answer, one she'd probably practiced a million times since he died. She laid down the jack of clubs. Dad threw an off-suit nine—my trick again. But something about her face was bothering me as I collected the pile. Her... *face*. I couldn't precisely identify what it was, but I was sure my father already had.

I pulled a diamond—none of my remaining cards were winners, though the game was the last thing on my mind. He'd been clear about what I needed to do: apply pressure, see if she breaks, see if she lies, see if she... *fits*. It had sounded like such a good idea before I was in a position to wield any kind of power. And the dizziness had not abated —worse now than it had been yesterday. I wasn't doing this right.

"Why did you lie about having a chainsaw?" I asked her. That was pressure, right? She'd lied about the broken toilet, too, but I understood that. Couldn't have me wandering into the corpse room.

Her hands stilled, her eyes locked on her cards. Finally, she tossed a diamond—the ace. Figured. "I wasn't sure what to tell you. I didn't know you were aware of Preston's... death." She lowered her cards and looked my way, an eyebrow raised.

I averted my gaze; I was staring. But I couldn't stop the interrogation, and by then I knew that's what it was. My losing ten and her winner, the ace of diamonds, glared from the tabletop. "What did you use to kill him?" I asked her.

She swallowed hard and glanced at my father. He nodded, so subtly that if I didn't know him well, I'd have missed it—*go ahead*. She turned back to me and waited until

I met her eyes once more. "The lamp. He came at me and..."

But her words were fading in my ears. Her eyelashes—that's what was different. She wasn't wearing eyeliner or mascara. Had she been wearing it at breakfast?

No. No she hadn't. I frowned, my heart ratcheting into overdrive. No makeup on the regular, yet she had been dolled up when we got here, her husband had even commented on it: *Are you wearing makeup?* Surprised. Broken flower stems—little clues. When we emerged from the woods in the middle of a storm, she had been expecting us.

I had missed something critical.

I suddenly wanted to go home, to sleep in my bed and forget this week had ever happened. But the pieces swirling in my head kept coming, snapping into place.

I've waited so long for this—what she'd said in the bedroom was not a thing you said to a one-night stand. And you certainly didn't plan to live with someone you'd just met. She had enough money to disappear on her own, and she was choosing my father. And now I thought I knew why. I thought I knew what I was missing. And maybe it was... good news.

So much hope. Yeah, yeah, I know.

I sat straighter as I asked: "So, how did you two meet?" Had he contacted her, seduced her after he realized that Preston was writing to me?

Her jaw dropped, but she recovered quickly and cocked her head at my father. He smiled at me, the biggest grin I'd seen on him since we arrived.

Success. My heart soared.

"You're a smart one, aren't you?" Her words were quiet, but there was no mistaking the hardness in her tone. This woman did not seem to appreciate that a child could see beyond her words. "It was just after my son died. I was in the market for a funeral home, and your father's place came highly recommended."

My father's place. We didn't have a funeral home, but that didn't require further explanation—my father could worm himself into any situation if he deemed it useful. But... they'd met when her son died? That was last winter, she'd said; eighteen months ago. I thought my father had brought me here because Preston was a pedophile—because he was writing to me. But I'd only been writing to Preston for four months.

My father had known Cherie long before I put pen to paper.

The room pulsed, wavering at the edges. This wasn't about my pen pal at all—we were here for *her*. My father had been involved with this woman, he'd waited until there was a storm on its way, and then he'd come up here to take her back with us.

Then... how was Preston writing to me? Was I wrong?

But that turtle. That stupid turtle stationery.

"Do you want me to come home with you, Poppy?" The cards hung limply in Cherie's hand. I set mine down, though my father kept his cards in his left hand, perusing them as Cherie talked. "I'd sure like to, Poppy, but your father has always been clear that I had to win you over first." The corners of her lips pulled up, her glittering eyes crinkling at the corners, but I found I couldn't return the smile. She'd known for a year that she had to impress me. And neither of them had tried to protect me from Preston. Was he writing me to get back at his wife? Was he writing me to get to my father? Did he think it was a game, figured he could get information on Dad from me? I imagined him capable of anything—Jeremy had seen it firsthand. Preston grinning while his wife and son stood sobbing in a lake of blood.

"Is she succeeding, Poppy? Is she winning you over?"

I startled and glanced at my father. Was this it? Had time run out? Either way, I thought I knew the right answer. She had killed her abusive pedophile husband to be with us, and she had money to help support us—enough to last forever. And now, she was doing her best to make me feel loved, to prove I would be as important as her own child had been. And my father wouldn't have brought me here if he didn't think it was good for us to meet. He'd been dating her for over a year. It didn't matter how he'd come to be involved with her, why he'd chosen her. Dad didn't waste his time. Ever. He wouldn't have wasted a year seducing a married woman for no reason. And he didn't need me here if it was just about money.

I was the most important thing in his world—this had all been for me.

I looked to her and back to my father, smiling. "Yes, Dad. She's succeeding."

Cherie beamed, but my father's eyes clouded. He leaned back in his chair and crossed one ankle over the opposite knee, but kept his gaze on mine. "Perhaps you're in a good mood because you slept so soundly all day, Poppy."

My lungs tightened.

"I was tired, I guess." What did a nap have to do with anything?

Children can't always see the full story without the breadth of experience gleaned through a life lived. My assessments during those days in the mountains were doomed to be based on half-truths. I was blind to the things I didn't know to look for.

"You were tired the night we moved Preston to the bathroom as well, yes?"

My stomach turned, the bile rancid and acidic—I could taste it in the back of my throat. These weren't small talk questions. I had made a mistake. But I had no idea what it was. "I... I guess so. But we'd done all that hiking..."

My father peeled a card from his hand and laid it on top of our diamonds: the ten of spades—trump. "Cherie, can I see the painkillers you gave my daughter?"

The air thinned. We both turned to face Cherie—his girlfriend for the last year or so. The reason that we'd come.

She sniffed. "They're Tylenol."

"What else is in it, Cherie? Codeine? Something to help her sleep?" He uncrossed his legs, leaned forward, and put his elbows on the table. "Did you put my daughter in danger?"

Was that why my world had been so hazy? She had put me to sleep so she could... have sex with my father?

Cherie had gone full statue. If a fly had landed on her eyeball, she would not have blinked. But then she shrugged one shoulder. This woman was controlled, practiced under pressure, maybe from her time working in a hospital, making life-and-death decisions. "I thought she needed to get some rest."

My back stiffened. No one was allowed to do things to my body unless I said it was okay—unless I enthusiastically consented. I might have grimaced through my father's sexual education speech, but I got the gist.

When she spoke again, her voice was higher—tight and insistent. "I gave her the right dosage, Carl. I'd *never* put Poppy in danger."

Carl? My dad's name was Steven. That was when I

realized I'd never heard her say his name—not once. Not even in the bedroom.

"If you wanted to keep my daughter safe, then why did you let your husband write her? And without a word to me about it."

Her eyes widened—desperate. "I didn't know! I swear! Preston must have figured out we were seeing each other and... I mean, who knows what he was thinking?"

Ah. I was right; the letters were just Preston screwing with the situation after the fact. Perhaps my father hadn't known initially, but he'd figured it out. Maybe he'd only realized Preston was writing me within the last few weeks—maybe that was why it had taken him so long to deal with it.

I swallowed hard to ease the burning in the back of my throat. I knew what my father wanted me to say, and I couldn't figure out another response that he'd accept. I had to make the right decision. If he thought I'd let someone get away with drugging me, he'd never trust me again. And that thought tightened every muscle in my abdomen, wringing the air from my lungs.

My father was watching me. "Poppy? You okay?"

"I was thinking about butterflies. How sometimes they break if you touch them." *If you put them under physical pressure.* It was the right answer, but I wanted to puke. The drugs, maybe. Just the drugs.

He turned to Cherie. And smiled.

She must have known then that she'd made a mistake. She should have seen it coming—people say that a lot. But that's always easy to say through the lens of hindsight.

"You should finish teaching Poppy to play the piano," my father said, his tone cold. "I've always liked Bach."

That's when the rain stopped.

I think my heart did too.

CHAPTER TWENTY

"You DON'T HAVE to do this," she whimpered.

But it was done. Maybe she should have tried to talk Dad out of it before he got the knots tied—not that she would have been successful. Now, she sat with her legs each attached to a separate length of rope that looped around the back of the instrument and connected to the opposite arm. She could stand, if she wanted, but she wasn't going anywhere unless she could move the entire piano. And if Dad wanted to, he could work her like a marionette from the far side of the grand.

My father seemed to have no interest in that. He leaned one shoulder against the wall, his arms crossed. "My daughter said you were going to teach her to play."

Tears were streaming down her cheeks when she brought her gaze to mine. I think I still believed there was hope, even then. As if somehow the pressure would make her stronger instead of breaking her. Sometimes rock shattered. Sometimes you got a diamond.

"Teach her, Cherie." His words were formed in ice that

I felt deep in my spine. "You made a promise to my daughter."

I sat glued to the bench, the rope rough where it snaked past my shins.

"Spread your fingers," Cherie said. Her voice shook. "Like this."

I did.

My therapist says that assaults to the psyche, the kind that make you question who you are, whether you're worth loving, can make your entire sense of self crumble. I've been told these are as bad as physical assaults.

But no one who says mental pain is the same as physical pain has seen what my father can do to a person.

We played. For hours and hours we played, as evening bled into night and faded into the wee morning. We played until my fingers were sore and my back ached. And still, I didn't stop playing. I knew what it meant if I stopped. And from the way she was playing, she did too.

Sometimes she cried, tears trailing down over the hollows in her cheeks, dripping off her chin. More often, she smiled through those tears. Proving that she could be with us. Proving that she was strong enough.

But that wasn't going to prove anything. And I think she knew it.

My father paced mostly, but sometimes he cut in when the melody faltered: "Do you have any other questions for her, Poppy?" He was providing the physical pressure. Was I supposed to handle the psychological?

I had no questions that would matter, of course, but I always came up with one. Despite the drugs, I could not forget how she'd wrapped my ankle so tenderly. How she'd helped me. If there was any chance that a question might tip the scales in her favor, I had to take it.

"What do you think we should do with Preston's body?" I asked. It was the kind of thing my father would ask if he wanted to know whether I understood, in an intimate way, the pressing matters—the matters of most concern. If I knew why broken flower stems meant threat. If I understood why it was bad to leave a screen sitting there outside the house. My face heated thinking about that screen.

"What do you think we should do?" One of her nails was torn; it left bloody fingerprints on the ivory, oozed out a tiny trail of red that trickled over the fine bones in her wrist.

"She asked you a question," my father said.

Cherie glanced at him, then back at me. Biding her time to come up with a good answer, though she had to have considered it before then. "Don't you worry, I'll take care of his body, and then all of this... it's ours. All ours. I already pulled the money out of the bank, just like..." She glanced at Dad again, eyes pleading as if to say *I did what you told me to, why are you doing this?*

So the money was hers then—her escape plan. She'd clearly believed it was safe, that I'd never look in the mattress if she didn't draw attention to it. I'd misinterpreted everything. She probably hid the pictures there to keep them from Preston... or as proof of his badness, should she ever need a reason for leaving. It was all part of a larger objective—to gain her freedom from him with enough cash to start over. But whether it had been Preston's money, whether it had been Cherie's, it was my father's now.

My dad cleared his throat. "Poppy deserves a straight answer." So calm. We might have been ordering takeout or having a conversation about lawn furniture.

Cherie bit her lip, then let out a long slow exhale. "I think we should bury him in the yard," she said finally.

My ribs constricted. You couldn't bury someone in your

own yard, and with the rocks here, I highly doubted it was possible to bury him deep enough that the animals wouldn't get at the corpse. My brow furrowed—disapproval, maybe, or worry for her. Her father should have taught her better. But my dad did not respond at all; he stared, face perfectly steady.

Cherie had not stopped playing, a series of haunting notes that reverberated through the living room and seeped into my veins. Chopin, I think, but I can't remember the tune now. At the time, I only knew it felt sad... if I were from the kind of family where sad was allowed.

"If you have a better idea, though, I'm happy to listen," Cherie said to me on breath that trembled in time to the melody. "I'd never disregard your opinion."

I've come to understand that applying the correct balance of pressure is critical in nearly every situation, but especially when dealing with people like my father. When someone is under too much pressure, they'll say absolutely anything to survive. They'll lie to your face. You can never trust a desperate person. And Dad could be heavy-handed. What I eventually did to him... I think he pushed me a little too hard. Even now I don't like to think about it.

But I was years from that back then. That night, I just had him.

And Cherie's raspy, panicked breath.

The nimble tinkling notes of that piano.

And my thoughts.

We watched the sun come up from the piano bench, a hazy golden glow that warmed the panes. Still some cloud cover, but the sky was clearing quickly. Soon, someone would try to contact Preston or his lovely wife; they were probably already working on the phone lines in the neighboring cities. How long until they realized the phones and electrical were out here?

I thought back to the box, the wires I had knocked askew. But if I had hit it hard enough to dislodge the phone wire, the others would have come out, too. And lightning certainly doesn't pull out a single wire.

Of course. She'd cut that line before we got here. She'd cut it so we had an excuse to stay. It was another broken stem that I should have noticed, that I would have noticed if I was half as good as I thought.

I dropped my hands from the keys, feeling like an irresponsible, ill-equipped child.

Which was exactly what I was.

A child with a responsibility I was in no way ready to handle.

I was as trapped as Cherie.

CHAPTER TWENTY-ONE

CHERIE SMILED LESS FREQUENTLY after my father laid down. He didn't go to the bedroom though; he lowered himself onto one of the couches in the living room with his head on one side, his boots propped up on the other, his arms crossed over his barrel chest. Within minutes, he was snoring.

The sun glinted on the windowpanes. A light drizzle spat on the windows, too, but the storm was fighting a losing battle. Just like Cherie.

She leaned her face closer to mine. "You can help me, Poppy," she whispered. "Please cut me loose."

From the outside, it was a simple choice—her one chance was while Dad was asleep, right? But others have a worldview steeped in the idea that people are mostly good, that hope prevails—that things work out for the best. For a child who knew, and indeed relied upon the monster beneath the bed, the available options were not so cut and dried.

In my place, most people would've reacted as I did; I have to believe that. No matter what they felt about it, even the most normal of humans would've gritted their teeth and gone along with his wishes, some more enthusiastically than others. What Cherie was asking me to do would not help her in the end. And the mere thought of betraying my father, of him no longer trusting me...

I guess that's hard to explain too. But when your father showers you with respect instead of hugs, you're loathe to give that up in the service of a woman who spiked your croissants with codeine.

But Cherie did not stop. "I can make it, Poppy. I know these woods better than your father. I'll bring back help."

But she wouldn't. There was a dead man in the bathroom. A man she'd killed. If I let her go, she'd run and never look back. She didn't even need the cash under the mattress —she had another stash somewhere, I was certain. An electronic one, since her husband was a tech guy. Or she'd stop at a bank, wipe out her credit cards. There was always another way out if you had money.

"Poppy, you can't let him kill me."

My father's snores echoed against the walls.

"I can help you," she hissed. "I can get you out of here— you can live with me. You aren't safe with him." She tugged the ropes; her wrists were raw, bleeding. "He'll do this to you eventually, too. I can't let that happen, now, can I?"

There were many things wrong with her logic, but the most glaring mistake was her notion that my father would ever hurt me. I understood what she was doing, though— she'd have said anything to convince me. Anything.

"*Poppy.*" Her eyes bored into me like those of the predator in the woods the night I hurt my ankle—maybe she had been there. Maybe she'd been watching even then. "Do you trust me?"

No. I only trusted my dad.

My father's snores caught, a single near-wakefulness hiccup, then went silent—listening?

Cherie seemed to be thinking the same because she glanced over at the living room, then lowered her fingers back to the piano and began playing once more—the duet she'd taught me. I raised my fingers and played along. C-C-E-E...

"I was always great at English, Poppy." Too loud—acting. For Dad, in case he was awake. "Once we get home to Alabama, I can teach you all kinds of things about storytelling. I know you want to be a writer, and I'm sure I can help you make that happen."

I tripped over the keys, a horrid, discordant noise. She was right, of course: being a writer was an idea I threw around sometimes. But only on paper.

I stopped playing, the tune forgotten. I could have believed my father had disclosed some unimportant detail about me—my career aspirations—for the sake of getting closer to her. But he didn't *know*. I had never said it aloud, not to anyone. And though my father knew about my pen pal, he didn't read the letters—I'd dropped most of those letters into the public mailbox near the school.

But Cherie... Not only did she know about those letters well before my father told her, but she'd read them. And the stationery... that tattoo...

"Was Preston ever in prison?" I asked.

"Prison?" She raised an eyebrow. But that was answer enough. That blue-ink prison tattoo I had seen on Preston's elbow had looked like faded ink because it *was* ink. Probably pen, washed out by the water in the tub. She'd drawn it on him, maybe to make my father connect that stationery to him—to drive home the idea that he was all bad, that he'd deserved to die.

It was smart, I guess. She'd known for a year that I was the one she had to convince. What better way to get into my head than by reading my letters? By asking me exactly what she needed to know?

I was never writing to Preston. I was writing to her.

She'd tricked me and my father both.

CHAPTER TWENTY-TWO

RUMINATING CAN BE DANGEROUS—YOU can think yourself in a circle. Proof is what matters, and by then I had all that I needed.

I'd had it all wrong from the beginning. I'd been writing to an entirely different person for months without realizing it. I hadn't noticed dozens of broken flower stems. Cherie had hidden the money—she'd hidden those dark drawings too. Had Cherie killed Jeremy? I couldn't prove it, and I knew she wouldn't admit it, but I thought she had.

And Preston... he'd kept his son's happier drawings in his desk. He hadn't wanted another child in Jeremy's shrine of a bedroom because he'd loved the boy. I'd probably misinterpreted the drawings altogether. Preston might've looked happy because he was the only one in the house who *was* happy. Preston smiling while Jeremy and his mother were in the dark, connected by terror and rage and that lake of red.

I knew what I had to do, but every time I raised my fingers, my ribs clenched so tightly it was hard to breathe. My stomach rolled in my abdomen, oily and sick. I needed to not be responsible. Not for what happened next. Especially since the decision had been made the moment my father tied her up.

Cherie had moved on to another song by then, high and in a major key, entirely too upbeat, like she was trying to buy her freedom with jubilance.

My father had resumed his snoring, replacing the dissipating grumble of far-off thunder. The sun had vanished behind the clouds again, but the rain was nothing more than an emaciated misting against the windows.

I took a breath, tried to speak, failed. Cherie appeared to have aged ten years, the wrinkles at the corners of her eyes more pronounced with her head turned to the side. I coughed, trying to clear the lump that had taken root in my throat, but the words still came out strangled. "You can't run."

The music stopped. Her pulse quickened. It seems a strange thing to have noticed in that moment, but I swear I saw it in the ridge of her throat, the frantic beating just below her jawline.

She turned to me with wide eyes. "Oh, I won't, Poppy. I swear I won't. I can make you and your father happy, I know I can."

No, you can't. You don't even want to. I could see the determination around her pupils, the fast way she was breathing. The way her muscles were tensing and relaxing —preparing for escape.

I tugged on the rope around her wrist, the one nearest me. The knots weren't especially complicated—they didn't need to be. She'd been held to the bench as much by fear as by the rope. Like me outside the tent, held down by pain more than the shoelace.

It was his snoring that did it, I think—his snoring made

her brave. The monster was asleep, and I was suddenly cooperating so he wouldn't wake to catch her. That was her opportunity. We both knew it.

But I knew more than she did.

"I'm really excited to have a mother," I said as her left wrist came loose. My voice felt too steady, but I was glad it wasn't shaking.

Cherie smiled, though it didn't reach her eyes. "I'm excited to have a daughter."

No mother should be able to lie like that. But they do.

The rope around Cherie's right wrist went slack, and she shifted, tugging at her right ankle. I bent to undo her left. Her body was trembling, the muscles beneath her flesh spastic with nervous energy. She was already running in her head. She was already running away from us.

From the next room, my father's grumbling stayed steady, the incessant roar of slumber.

And then... she was free.

I righted myself as Cherie pushed herself to standing and stumbled away from the piano. Was there any woman who'd have stayed sitting on that bench with me? It was no choice at all.

She took another stumbling step backward.

"You said you wouldn't run," I said, so quietly I could barely hear the words over the rumble of my father's snoring. I do wonder what would have happened if she'd stayed sitting after she was untied. But I'll never know.

She blinked, but her eyes were not on me—I was already invisible. I should have felt something about that, about being so easy to discard, but I don't remember. Life's always easier if you can forget the pain.

Cherie turned on her heel and fled, and in five sharp beats, she was at the red-stained front door. I can still hear the wet slapping of her bare feet on the wood. The gruff way the lock popped, then the knob, letting in a gush of wind and the thin patter of diminished drizzling.

The sheet music caught the breeze, lifted from the piano, and shuddered to the floor with a noise like that of the crows in the logging yard. I think I stood then. I can't remember. But I do know I was standing when I realized that the steady grumbling had stopped. The pages were scattered across the hardwoods.

By the time I turned back to the living room, my father was standing in front of the couch, his arms crossed, his hunting blade clenched in his fist. He glanced at me, then the loose ropes. He shook his head, but his lips were shiny pink, fine bubbles of spittle tucked into the corners. Had he always foamed at the mouth like that when he was brimming with anticipation? Had it only been hidden beneath his beard?

To this day, I don't know. I never saw him without his beard again.

"She lied to us, Dad."

He nodded. He already knew. He'd been trying to... teach me. His eyes stayed locked on the open front door, his knuckles white around the blade. "You made the right choice."

Had I? I wasn't even sure what I'd chosen outside deciding not to act. But I've since come to learn that inaction *is* an action. And often a profound one.

"Sometimes, butterflies act a little too bravely when you let them go," he said, hurrying across the wood toward the open door. "That's what gets them eaten."

CHAPTER TWENTY-THREE

THAT MIGHT HAVE BEEN the first time I saw my father run. It didn't occur to me then that he'd never had to give chase before, that he'd never had a reason.

But that day, he flew like he had lightning on his heels.

I stumbled after him, my hip hitting the piano with a crack, my injured foot jolting against the floor with what should have been an electric burst of pain. But I didn't react to it. I barely felt it, just a weird far-off ache.

I was a moth attracted to the light. I was a magnet pulled toward the opposite pole.

I was a daughter who needed to see.

I wish I could tell you that I acted bravely, that I ran from the house and over the lawn, screaming his name. That I tried to save her.

But I had already used the only tactics I knew.

We had tested her, and she had failed in every conceivable way.

And so had I.

He caught up with her a third of the way across the lawn. She was tired, I'm sure, or her legs had fallen asleep.

And to assume she'd beat him barefoot in a race when he'd kept his boots on... I doubted she'd even noticed that, that he'd lain down with his boots still tied up tight. Boots were for people who wanted to be prepared. People who were listening for the right moment to put those boots on the ground.

But Cherie had not noticed what she didn't want to see —to notice the boots meant losing hope. Most make stupid decisions when they're panicked, when they're so singularly focused that they can't see what's right in front of them. I think that was why my father taught me to rein in the fear from the time I was born.

There was no room for panic or error in our lives.

No space to be afraid.

Because if I had the capacity to be afraid of anything, I'd most certainly be afraid of him. Better to scrape the fear out of me entirely.

So, I guess I wasn't afraid while I stood framed in the carved doorway. I was probably numb—the snippets of memory that come back to me from time to time are laced with a profound detachment, as if I were always watching it happen to someone else.

I stared out across the sloping front yard. The drizzling rain made her figure waver, but her voice did not; her screams were louder than the rain, louder than my heart-beat, pulsing in my ears.

"Help! Someone, help! Please!"

To this day, I'm not sure who she was calling out to. It was a mile to the driveway—to the road—and even if by some miracle passerby had heard her, they would never have gotten to her in time. It was twenty miles to another home, more private than our place in Riverside. And no one ever heard the screaming from our house.

No one but me.

I leaned into the wind, every jolt of her running feet against the lawn making her wailing halt—a series of hiccuping shrieks.

I remember wanting to call to her, to egg her on, wondering if she might be able to make it to the road. But even if she did, there'd be no one to help her. And I knew better anyway. My father had planned this—he'd brought us here. He hadn't even told her his real name.

She was going to die from the moment we left our house in Alabama.

My hands were claws against the doorframe. I could feel splinters beneath my fingernails, the pressure peeling the nails back in a way that was both uncomfortable and invigorating; it held me to myself as she barreled toward the trees. My heart thundered in my ears, though I didn't feel it in the rest of my body. I was an observer only. Helpless. Disconnected.

But I couldn't look away. I didn't think I'd earned the right to look away.

And I didn't want to be a child forced to make decisions that someone else dictated. I wanted to have control over the questions too.

Doesn't everyone?

So, I stared while her hair flew behind her, tendrils of honey-blond darkened by the waning drizzle. For a split second, I was her, my breath panting from my lungs, the evergreen brush barreling toward me, a predator closing in at my back. *Almost there. Almost.* The sun blinked out from behind the clouds, a single ray of pure hope glittering against the tree line, marking the way forward.

And then she was falling, cut down in an instant. She didn't even stumble—one moment she was up, running, and the next she was spread-eagled on the lawn. My breath left my lungs in the same moment, and I felt the jolt in my ribs as I had felt it outside the tent when I hurt my ankle, a violent *thwack* that stole my air.

My father was on her in a heartbeat, yanking her up by that honey-gold hair as the sun once again slipped behind the clouds. She screamed louder, but the timbre was strange, a low staccato type of scream, broken differently than it was when she was running. *Ah-ah-ah-ah.*

Staccato. Cherie had taught me that word.

The sun blinked on again, so bright I squinted. And that's when I saw the rainbow emerge from her neck, though there was no green or yellow or violet. The only color was crimson, a beating, pulsing arc of blood.

But the screaming... how was she still screaming with blood spurting from her neck?

And then I knew. I knew exactly what that sound was. When he dropped her to the lawn and raised his face to the brilliant sky, my father was still laughing.

CHAPTER TWENTY-FOUR

I PULLED myself away from the doorway then and went about cleaning up... I think. It's hazy now, memory that I can't quite tap into, no matter how hard I try. I'd been up all night with Cherie, so I imagine I wouldn't have been firing on all cylinders, as my pen pal might have said. I'd miss talking to her in the months that followed. I suppose I was lucky to have had that brief time to pour my heart out on the page before it all fell apart.

I do remember that I unwound the rope from the piano. I sat there on the bench, holding it, trying not to listen to my father's footsteps on the hardwoods, the slamming of doors, the squeal of drawer hinges. There were birds, too, chittering from the trees. It wasn't raining anymore, but I pretended it was. I think I wanted the lawn to end up clean.

I don't remember deciding to play, but I recall doing it at some point—C-C, E-E, A-A, C-C... Without the higher part of the duet, the music fell flat, and when I looked up, my father was standing in the doorway, that manila envelope in his hand. The music stopped.

That was the last time I played an instrument. The very last.

"You have blood on your sock," he said.

I looked down. One drop, a single drop. From her fingertip, her bleeding nail. "Okay."

That was it. It was all I had in me. And there was a strong smell in the air, one so pungent that I couldn't believe I hadn't noticed it before. My eyes watered. My nose itched —burned.

"Come on, Poppy. We have work to do."

Things go black here, a yawning void where most people would keep memories. Probably better that way. I mostly remember staring at the living room without really seeing it, a blurred mass of amorphous shapes—not exactly book fodder.

I was still staring when he picked me up, his arm beneath my knees, cradling me against his chest as he had on the way to the house—only three days earlier, but it felt like a lifetime. I clung to him and watched the sky as he carried me outside and down the front steps and across the lawn.

"I've got you, Poppy. It's not far to the tent. And there's a shortcut to the truck." I leaned my head against his chest. His jacket—Preston's raincoat—was lumpy and uncomfortable, the fabric hard, broken in a uniform pattern. The money. He'd tucked it into his coat. More than what I'd found, though—much more.

But I was too tired to care. Blinking felt like someone was abrading my eyeballs with sandpaper. I inhaled deeply and gagged. That smell. But I recognized it then: gasoline. On his clothes, on his hands, maybe on me too.

"I wish we got to see the waterfall, Dad."

"I'll take you to as many waterfalls as you want once you're healed."

"Okay." But he never did. I never wanted to see a waterfall again.

He stopped. Had I fallen asleep? Were we at the campsite already? I lifted my head and squinted through the vibrant morning.

We were still on the lawn, where Cherie had died, but all that was left of her was a muddy brown stain on the storm-soaked grass.

"She was going to leave him," my father said. Where had he put her body?

"She cleaned out all their bank accounts. He found out, cut her throat for it. He felt bad though, as I imagine anyone would. He slit his wrists, then tossed a match. Burned this whole place to the ground with them inside. All that money gone, too. What a waste."

He was giving me a story, an explanation, not that it would ever come up. No one ever came looking for us. No one would ever know we'd been here.

"She was going to leave him," I repeated. "That's very sad."

"I'll make sure you never have that kind of sadness," he said.

"I don't have a pen pal anymore. That's a little sad."

He peered down at me, eyes narrowed. "You never had a pen pal."

"I never had a pen pal," I said. But I had. I'd never be able to tell anyone about him, though. Johnny wasn't real anyway.

Dad took two more steps, then three. In the sunlight, I could see the puddles of gasoline, shimmering with iridescent destruction. "Do you want to do the honors? The matches are in my shirt pocket, and my arms are full." He tensed his biceps, jiggling me.

Beyond him, the windows were already orange with flames, swelling like a burgeoning sunset from inside. Black smoke curled from the open door and up toward the cerulean sky. And when I strained my ears and listened, I could hear it—the crackle of fire. My gaze dropped to the lawn, to the place where he'd killed her. The greasy puddles of accelerant.

"Poppy?"

I nodded and slipped the matches from his pocket.

"Good girl."

The lawn went up with a *whoosh*. The crackle as the flames raced over the lawn and back toward the house was deafening, though I don't think it could have been as loud as I recall.

"Everything will be fine now, Poppy."

I nodded and settled my head against his coat, the bundled cash. My father had never lied to me. He couldn't. I knew him better than anyone, and the thing I knew most about him was that he would always, *always* protect me. I was his world, and he was the sunset bleeding color from the landscape until it all goes dark. He'd always do what was right.

For me. Everyone else be damned.

I clung to his shoulders, and we made our way toward the forest. The last I saw of the house, once so proud against the cliff's face, was the blackened front door, the living room a raging ball of crimson.

I closed my eyes.

And slept.

CHAPTER TWENTY-FIVE

POPPY, NOW

I SUPPOSE this is a story about the first time I tried to save myself. Saved is a strong word, perhaps—hyperbole used to suggest that I intentionally, and with an extraordinary amount of foresight, decided at nine years old to escape my father. To escape from all the slippery bloody things that keep humans up at night. But I never had the luxury of being squeamish—never had the luxury of fearful insomnia. To embrace those feelings while living in that house... I'd never have slept again.

So yes, I absorbed those few days in the mountains as I absorbed most things from that time—unquestioningly. It had to be done.

But acclimation doesn't always mean acceptance. We all do what we have to do to survive. You'd have done the same, though you'll have to trust me on that, since I'm neither inclined to prove it nor do I have the ability to put you mind-and-body into the skin of a child watching her daddy do horrific things. But I imagine that somewhere, deep down, you already know it's true. You'd kill a lion if it came at you. You'd shoot your own dog if it meant your life.

And every incremental sliver of growth means killing pieces of yourself, smothering the things you can no longer accommodate within your psyche. Adapting lets you live another day, and more than that, it forces you to grow into a new, better version of yourself.

It doesn't even require blood under your fingernails.

Unless, of course, you're me.

Want more Poppy? Her saga is far from over.
Continue the Born Bad series with
***Deadly Words*—grab it on**
MEGHANOFLYNN.COM,
then read on for a sneak peek!

"BRILLIANT, DARK, AND IMPOSSIBLE TO PUT DOWN,
POPPY IS UNFORGETTABLE—UNLIKE ANY
CHARACTER YOU'VE READ BEFORE.
THIS IS STORYTELLING AT ITS FINEST."
~*BESTSELLING AUTHOR EMERALD O'BRIEN*

PRAISE FOR BESTSELLING AUTHOR
MEGHAN O'FLYNN

"Creepy and haunting...fully immersive thrillers. The Ash Park series should be everyone's next binge-read."
~*New York Times Bestselling Author Andra Watkins*

"Full of complex, engaging characters and evocative detail, *Wicked Sharp* is a white-knuckle thrill ride. O'Flynn is a master storyteller."
~*Paul Austin Ardoin, USA Today Bestselling Author*

"Nobody writes with such compelling and entrancing prose as O'Flynn. With perfectly executed twists, Born Bad is chilling, twisted, heart-pounding suspense. This is my new favorite thriller series."
~*Bestselling Author Emerald O'Brien*

"Visceral, fearless, and addictive, this series will keep you on the edge of your seat."
~*Bestselling Author Mandi Castle*

"Intense and suspenseful...captured me from
the first chapter and held me enthralled
until the final page."
~*Susan Sewell, Reader's Favorite*

"Cunning, delightfully disturbing, and
addictive, the Ash Park series is an
expertly written labyrinth of twisted,
unpredictable awesomeness!"
~*Award-winning Author Beth Teliho*

"Dark, gritty, and raw, O'Flynn's work will take
your mind prisoner and keep you awake
far into the morning hours."
~*Bestselling Author Kristen Mae*

"From the feverishly surreal to the downright
demented, O'Flynn takes you on a twisted
journey through the deepest and darkest
corners of the human mind."
~*Bestselling Author Mary Widdicks*

"With unbearable tension and gripping, thought-provoking storytelling, O'Flynn explores fear in all the best—and creepiest— ways. Masterful psychological thrillers replete with staggering, unpredictable twists."
~Bestselling Author Wendy Heard

LEARN MORE AT MEGHANOFLYNN.COM

DEADLY WORDS

A Born Bad Novel

CHAPTER 1

The name's Poppy, Poppy Pratt, and I'm at your service, though I'll be the first to admit that I'm not always so agreeable.

It's in my nature I suppose, and always has been—that fire I keep hidden within me is in my blood. Dad says it's like air, like water, anything that sits there unnoticed until you don't have it anymore. I don't have a single reason to disbelieve him.

I think we're all one step from a storm if we don't get what we need, but I guess that makes it sound more intense than it is. You won't find maniacs here, frothing at the mouth—we aren't those people.

Maniac adjacent, maybe, but only if you believe the gossip around town. The gossip is not about us, though; it's never about us. It's about the "deserters"—the folks who leave this or any of the other nearby towns looking for something better. This is the kind of place people move on from —they find a job, they find love, they drive away as fast as they can. It's not a shock that anyone might up and disappear, so most of the gossips cluck their tongues, but they don't worry about the deserters. They don't know they should.

I know more than most people. I can read the high school books, even if I'm not allowed to in my elementary classes, and the education I get at home...well, that's a different kind of smart.

I rest my elbows on the railing of our narrow back porch, the wood already wet, little slivers embedding themselves in my forearms. I like the way it feels, damp and prickly—like *something*. *Thrashy*. I made that word up when I was smaller to describe the way some things get through your defenses against your will, stabbing at your soft spots. I don't think my father likes the word much. That's why he bought me a dictionary, then a thesaurus. He doesn't like anything he's on the outside of, and here, in this house, the things you don't know can be dangerous.

I press my arms harder against the wood, letting the slivers prick, letting them stab—*thrashy, thrashy, thrashy*. Acres of glistening grass stare back at me. Beyond the green, the sky cuts the horizon with a wound of deep indigo that looks like a mark left by a good whipping. I wouldn't know from personal experience—my father would *never* hit me— but almost every other child I know bears the scars of their parents' rage. It's no wonder people leave here.

The wood of the shed is damp, too, I can tell by the darker color along the slab. What little remains of twilight glows against the west-facing boards and paints the roses that bloom around the building with a grayed blush of color. The single window is a hazy black.

The wind brushes silky fingers through my hair, but there's electricity in the clouds tonight—not just rain. We're going to get a storm. Just as well—it happens all the time down here in Alabama, one hurricane after another some years—but this'll be a soupy wet trek toward a flood, and that's worse than the wind. Torrential rains took out our shed one year, the water rising over the concrete slab, picking up the lower boards like it was going to lift the thing clean off like a newfangled Noah's Ark. I stood in the doorway, Dad's arm warm at my side, and imagined myself climbing aboard, my blond curls like corkscrews in the breeze, setting sail for somewhere else. Anywhere else.

That was a bad year. Until we rebuilt the shed. That's the thing about life, about all things that fall apart, that crumble under pressure: they can't stay crumbled. Not when they're up against me. Nature gave me glue, too, and I don't break easy.

I blink. The light in the shed goes on, and the glass of the single window glares at me from the other side of the yard, the path to the shed glowing a hazy reddish-orange. Tepid. Watered-down.

It still looks like blood.

GET *DEADLY WORDS* AT MEGHANOFLYNN.COM!

"BRILLIANT, DARK, AND IMPOSSIBLE TO PUT DOWN. O'FLYNN MASTERFULLY CRAFTS A TWISTED TALE OF BURIED SECRETS IN *DEADLY WORDS*. POPPY IS UNFORGETTABLE—UNLIKE ANY CHARACTER YOU'VE READ BEFORE. THIS IS STORYTELLING AT ITS FINEST."

~*BESTSELLING AUTHOR EMERALD O'BRIEN*

FAMISHED

An Ash Park Novel

Focus, or she's dead.

Petrosky ground his teeth together, but it didn't stop the panic from swelling hot and frantic within him. After the arrest last week, this crime should have been fucking impossible.

He wished it were a copycat. He knew it wasn't.

Anger knotted his chest as he examined the corpse that lay in the middle of the cavernous living room. Dominic Harwick's intestines spilled onto the white marble floor as though someone had tried to run off with them. His eyes were wide, milky at the edges already, so it had been awhile since someone gutted his sorry ass and turned him into a rag doll in a three-thousand-dollar suit.

That rich prick should have been able to protect her.

Petrosky looked at the couch: luxurious, empty, cold. Last week Hannah had sat on that couch, staring at him with wide green eyes that made her seem older than her twenty-three years. She had been happy, like Julie had been before she was stolen from him. He pictured Hannah as she might have been at eight years old, skirt twirling, dark hair flying, face flushed with sun, like one of the photos of Julie he kept tucked in his wallet.

They all started so innocent, so pure, so...*vulnerable*.

The idea that Hannah was the catalyst in the deaths of eight others, the cornerstone of some serial killer's plan, had not occurred to him when they first met. But it had later. It did now.

Petrosky resisted the urge to kick the body and refocused on the couch. Crimson congealed along the white leather as if marking Hannah's departure.

He wondered if the blood was hers.

The click of a doorknob caught Petrosky's attention. He turned to see Bryant Graves, the lead FBI agent, entering the room from the garage door, followed by four other agents. Petrosky tried not to think about what might be in the garage. Instead, he watched the four men survey the living room from different angles, their movements practically choreographed.

"Damn, does everyone that girl knows get whacked?" one of the agents asked.

"Pretty much," said another.

A plain-clothed agent stooped to inspect a chunk of scalp on the floor. Whitish-blond hair waved, tentacle-like, from the dead skin, beckoning Petrosky to touch it.

"You know this guy?" one of Graves's cronies asked from the doorway.

"Dominic Harwick." Petrosky nearly spat out the bastard's name.

"No signs of forced entry, so one of them knew the killer," Graves said.

"*She* knew the killer," Petrosky said. "Obsession builds over time. This level of obsession indicates it was probably someone she knew well."

But who?

Petrosky turned back to the floor in front of him, where words scrawled in blood had dried sickly brown in the morning light.

> Ever drifting down the stream—
> Lingering in the golden gleam—
> Life, what is it but a dream?

Petrosky's gut clenched. He forced himself to look at Graves. "And, Han—" *Hannah*. Her name caught in his throat, sharp like a razor blade. "The girl?"

"There are bloody drag marks heading out to the back shower and a pile of bloody clothes," Graves said. "He must have cleaned her up before taking her. We've got the techs on it now, but they're working the perimeter first." Graves bent and used a pencil to lift the edge of the scalp, but it was suctioned to the floor with dried blood.

"Hair? That's new," said another voice. Petrosky didn't bother to find out who had spoken. He stared at the coppery stains on the floor, his muscles twitching with anticipation. Someone could be tearing her apart as the agents roped off the room. How long did she have? He wanted to run, to find her, but he had no idea where to look.

"Bag it," Graves said to the agent examining the scalp, then turned to Petrosky. "It's all been connected from the beginning. Either Hannah Montgomery was his target all along or she's just another random victim. I think the fact that she isn't filleted on the floor like the others points to her being the goal, not an extra."

"He's got something special planned for her," Petrosky whispered. He hung his head, hoping it wasn't already too late.

If it was, it was all his fault.

GET *FAMISHED* AT MEGHANOFLYNN.COM.

"FEARLESS, SMART WRITING, AND A PLOT
THAT WILL STICK WITH YOU."
~*AWARD-WINNING AUTHOR BETH TELIHO*

SHADOW'S KEEP

**Graybell, Mississippi is the perfect,
quiet little down.
That silence is about to be broken.**

CHAPTER 1

For William Shannahan, six-thirty on Tuesday, the third of August, was "the moment." Life was full of those moments, his mother had always told him, experiences that prevented you from going back to who you were before, tiny decisions that changed you forever.

And that morning, the moment came and went, though he didn't recognize it, nor would he ever have wished to recall that morning again for as long as he lived. But he would never, from that day on, be able to forget it.

He left his Mississippi farmhouse a little after six, dressed in running shorts and an old T-shirt that still had sunny yellow paint dashed across the front from decorating the child's room. *The child.* William had named him Brett, but he'd never told anyone that. To everyone else, the baby was just that-thing-you-could-never-mention, particularly since William had also lost his wife at Bartlett General.

His green Nikes beat against the gravel, a blunt metronome as he left the porch and started along the road parallel to the Oval, what the townsfolk called the near hundred square miles of woods that had turned marshy wasteland when freeway construction had dammed the creeks downstream. Before William was born, those fifty or so unlucky folks who owned property inside the Oval had gotten some settlement from the developers when their houses flooded and were deemed uninhabitable. Now those homes were part of a ghost town, tucked well beyond the reach of prying eyes.

William's mother had called it a disgrace. William thought it might be the price of progress, though he'd never dared to tell her that. He'd also never told her that his fondest memory of the Oval was when his best friend Mike had beat the crap out of Kevin Pultzer for punching William in the eye. That was before Mike was the sheriff, back when they were all just "us" or "them" and William had always been a them, except when Mike was around. He might fit in somewhere else, some other place where the rest of the dorky goofballs lived, but here in Graybel he was just a little...odd. Oh well. People in this town gossiped far too much to trust them as friends anyway.

William sniffed at the marshy air, the closely-shorn grass sucking at his sneakers as he increased his pace. Somewhere near him a bird shrieked, sharp and high. He startled as it took flight above him with another aggravated scream.

Straight ahead, the car road leading into town was bathed in filtered dawn, the first rays of sun painting the gravel gold, though the road was slippery with moss and morning damp. To his right, deep shadows pulled at him from the trees; the tall pines crouched close together as if hiding a secret bundle in their underbrush. Dark but calm, quiet—comforting. Legs pumping, William headed off the road toward the pines.

A snap like that of a muted gunshot echoed through the morning air, somewhere deep inside the wooded stillness, and though it was surely just a fox, or maybe a raccoon, he paused, running in place, disquiet spreading through him like the worms of fog that were only now rolling out from under the trees to be burned off as the sun made its debut. Cops never got a moment off, although in this sleepy town the worst he'd see today would be an argument over cattle. He glanced up the road. Squinted. Should he continue up the brighter main street or escape into the shadows beneath the trees?

That was his moment.

William ran toward the woods.

As soon as he set foot inside the tree line, the dark descended on him like a blanket, the cool air brushing his face as another hawk shrieked overhead. William nodded to it, as if the animal had sought his approval, then swiped his arm over his forehead and dodged a limb, pick-jogging his way down the path. A branch caught his ear. He winced. Six foot three was great for some things, but not for running in the woods. Either that or God was pissed at him, which wouldn't be surprising, though he wasn't clear on what he had done wrong. Probably for smirking at his memories of Kevin Pultzer with a torn T-shirt and a bloodied nose.

He smiled again, just a little one this time.

When the path opened up, he raised his gaze above the canopy. He had an hour before he needed to be at the precinct, but the pewter sky beckoned him to run quicker before the heat crept up. It was a good day to turn forty-two, he decided. He might not be the best-looking guy around, but he had his health. And there was a woman whom he adored, even if she wasn't sure about him yet.

William didn't blame her. He probably didn't deserve her, but he'd surely try to convince her that he did, like he had with Marianna...though he didn't think weird card tricks would help this time. But weird was what he had. Without it, he was just background noise, part of the wallpaper of this small town, and at forty-one—*no, forty-two, now*—he was running out of time to start over.

He was pondering this when he rounded the bend and saw the feet. Pale soles barely bigger than his hand, poking from behind a rust-colored boulder that sat a few feet from the edge of the trail. He stopped, his heart throbbing an erratic rhythm in his ears.

Please let it be a doll. But he saw the flies buzzing around the top of the boulder. Buzzing. Buzzing.

William crept forward along the path, reaching for his hip where his gun usually sat, but he touched only cloth. The dried yellow paint scratched his thumb. He thrust his hand into his pocket for his lucky coin. No quarter. Only his phone.

William approached the rock, the edges of his vision dark and unfocused as if he were looking through a telescope, but in the dirt around the stone he could make out deep paw prints. Probably from a dog or a coyote, though these were *enormous*—nearly the size of a salad plate, too big for anything he'd expect to find in these woods. He frantically scanned the underbrush, trying to locate the animal, but saw only a cardinal appraising him from a nearby branch.

Someone's back there, someone needs my help.

He stepped closer to the boulder. *Please don't let it be what I think it is.* Two more steps and he'd be able to see beyond the rock, but he could not drag his gaze from the trees where he was certain canine eyes were watching. Still nothing there save the shaded bark of the surrounding woods. He took another step—cold oozed from the muddy earth into his shoe and around his left ankle, like a hand from the grave. William stumbled, pulling his gaze from the trees just in time to see the boulder rushing at his head and then he was on his side in the slimy filth to the right of the boulder, next to...

Oh god, oh god, oh god.

William had seen death in his twenty years as a deputy, but usually it was the result of a drunken accident, a car wreck, an old man found dead on his couch.

This was not that. The boy was no more than six, probably less. He lay on a carpet of rotting leaves, one arm draped over his chest, legs splayed haphazardly as if he, too, had tripped in the muck. But this wasn't an accident; the boy's throat was torn, jagged ribbons of flesh peeled back, drooping on either side of the muscle meat, the unwanted skin on a Thanksgiving turkey. Deep gouges permeated his chest and abdomen, black slashes against mottled green flesh, the wounds obscured behind his shredded clothing and bits of twigs and leaves.

William scrambled backward, clawing at the ground, his muddy shoe kicking the child's ruined calf, where the boy's shy white bones peeked from under congealing blackish tissue. The legs looked...*chewed on.*

His hand slipped in the muck. The child's face was turned to his, mouth open, black tongue lolling as if he were about to plead for help. *Not good, oh shit, not good.*

William finally clambered to standing, yanked his cell from his pocket, and tapped a button, barely registering his friend's answering bark. A fly lit on the boy's eyebrow above a single white mushroom that crept upward over the landscape of his cheek, rooted in the empty socket that had once contained an eye.

"Mike, it's William. I need a...tell Dr. Klinger to bring the wagon."

He stepped backward, toward the path, shoe sinking again, the mud trying to root him there, and he yanked his foot free with a squelching sound. Another step backward and he was on the path, and another step off the path again, and another, another, feet moving until his back slammed against a gnarled oak on the opposite side of the trail. He jerked his head up, squinting through the greening awning half convinced the boy's assailant would be perched there, ready to leap from the trees and lurch him into oblivion on flensing jaws. But there was no wretched animal. Blue leaked through the filtered haze of dawn.

William lowered his gaze, Mike's voice a distant crackle irritating the edges of his brain but not breaking through—he could not understand what his friend was saying. He stopped trying to decipher it and said, "I'm on the trails behind my house, found a body. Tell them to come in through the path on the Winchester side." He tried to listen to the receiver, but heard only the buzzing of flies across the trail—had they been so loud a moment ago? Their noise grew, amplified to unnatural volumes, filling his head until every other sound fell away—was Mike still talking? He pushed *End,* pocketed the phone, and then leaned back and slid down the tree trunk.

And William Shannahan, not recognizing the event the rest of his life would hinge upon, sat at the base of a gnarled oak tree on Tuesday, the third of August, put his head into his hands, and wept.

GET *SHADOW'S KEEP* ON MEGHANOFLYNN.COM.

"MASTERFUL, STAGGERING, TWISTED... AND COMPLETELY UNPREDICTABLE."
~BESTSELLING AUTHOR WENDY HEARD

WANT MORE FROM MEGHAN?

There are many more books to choose from!

Learn more about Meghan's novels on
https://meghanoflynn.com

ABOUT THE AUTHOR

With books deemed "visceral, haunting, and fully immersive" (*New York Times bestseller, Andra Watkins*), Meghan O'Flynn has made her mark on the thriller genre. Meghan is a clinical therapist who draws her character inspiration from her knowledge of the human psyche. She is the bestselling author of gritty crime novels and serial killer thrillers, all of which take readers on the dark, gripping, and unputdownable journey for which Meghan is notorious. Learn more at https://meghanoflynn.com! While you're there, join Meghan's reader group, and get a **FREE SHORT STORY** just for signing up.

Want to connect with Meghan?
https://meghanoflynn.com

Made in the USA
Middletown, DE
30 April 2022

65024564R00102